# Swift Horse

# PRAISE FOR THE MUSTANG MOUNTAIN SERIES

I looooove horses and barrel racing. And I love Mustang Mountain!
When I brought home #5 and #6 from school I couldn't put them down.
—An enthusiastic reader, Naomi

I love your books and would rather read them than watch TV.
They also have adventure and that's perfect for me.
—#1 fan, Laurel

Your books rock! I have every one of them except the new one (#7 *Free Horse*).
Your books rule!!!!!!!!!! I've always loved 2 write but reading your books
makes me wanna write more. When I get older I hope to become
an awesome author just like you.
—Your #1 fan, Jess

WOW! ... You write the best stories ever! ...
I love how you have the stories so real and I hope that you write
some more amazing books for Mustang Mountain. You'd make myself and
all of my friends very happy.
—Kaylan

I love horses and I really want one, but I can't.
So I read about them and last spring I read your books and I LOVED them.
—From one of your fans, Tori

I couldn't wait to read *Free Horse*, but my parents said that I had to wait
till my birthday. While I was waiting I reread one to six of Mustang Mountain.
It took me one day to read *Free Horse*, but it was awesome.
I can't wait till your next one.
—Lauren

(Sharon writes back to all the fans who write to her at her email address:
sharon@sharonsiamon.com. Join the crowd!)

**8**

MUSTANG MOUNTAIN

# Swift Horse

**Sharon Siamon**

Edited by Lori Burwash
Proofread by Elizabeth McLean
Cover photos by Michael E. Burch (mountains)
    and Douglas Kent Hall/ZUMA/Corbis, "The Cowboy Spirit" (horse)
Cover design by Roberta Batchelor
Interior design by Margaret Lee / Bamboo & Silk Design Inc.

Printed and bound in Canada.

**Library and Archives Canada Cataloguing in Publication**
Siamon, Sharon
    Swift horse / Sharon Siamon.
    (Mustang Mountain ; 8)
For children aged 8-12.
ISBN 1-55285-659-3
    1. Horses—Juvenile fiction. I. Title. II. Series: Mustang Mountain ; 8.
    PS8587.I225S95 2005    jC813'.54    C2005-900563-7

The publisher acknowledges the support of the Canada Council and the
Cultural Services Branch of the Government of British Columbia in
making this publication possible. Whitecap Books also acknowledges the
financial support of the Government of Canada through the Book Publishing
Industry Development Program for our publishing activities.

Please note: Some places mentioned in this book are fictitious
while others are not.

The inside pages of this book are 100% recycled, processed chlorine-free
paper with 40% post-consumer content. For more information, visit
Markets Initiative's website: www.oldgrowthfree.com.

*To Ila Morning Camara*

# CONTENTS

# ACKNOWLEDGMENTS

I'd like to thank the following people for helping me with the research and writing of this book.

Lisa Scarlett, Ontario Barrel Racing Association President, for her wonderful tales of barrel racing horses and for reading a draft of *Swift Horse*.

Chelsea L'Hirondelle for information about young barrel racers in Alberta and for sharing her personal story.

Dr. Wayne Burwash for his advice on horses and their injuries.

And, as ever, Lori Burwash for her thoughtful edit, inspiring comments and good horse sense.

# CHAPTER 1

# BAD NEWS

Alison Chant stared at the telephone message in her hand.

"You can't do this to me!" she shouted into the silence of the Mustang Mountain Ranch kitchen. Her cry echoed back from the high ceiling.

Seconds later, her cousin Becky Sandersen banged through the ranch house door and skidded into the kitchen. "Alison? I heard yelling. Are you okay?"

"No, I'm not okay." Alison thrust the message at Becky. "Read this." She watched her cousin's brown eyes widen as she read the news.

"This is awful." Becky glanced up at her slender, dark-haired cousin. "Your parents aren't getting back together like they said."

"Can you believe it?" Alison's voice was high and scornful. "They didn't even have the nerve to tell me in person. They left a message with Slim, the cook."

"It's hard to get through to the ranch on the radio-phone." Becky started to make excuses.

"They could have tried a little harder." Alison shook her head. "My parents treat me like I'm some kind of suitcase they left in storage. First, Dad couldn't take me to Paris in July—even though he promised—because he and Mom were in couples therapy. Fine, so they shipped me here to Mustang Mountain, where nobody, including you, was glad to see me."

Becky's normally rosy cheeks flushed a deeper red. "That's not true!"

"Yes, it is, and you know it," Alison rushed on, "but I didn't care because my parents were getting together again. I could live in my old house in New York, be near my friend Meg, go back to our old school. I even gave you my horse, my Shadow, because I was going home."

She grabbed the note back from Becky and smacked it with her hand. "And now this. I'm not going home. My whole life is unraveling like a cheap sweater!"

"I'm sorry ..." Becky could see that behind Alison's scornful face, she was trembling with hurt and anger. Her cousin could go from an elegant, poised fifteen-year-old to a spoiled five-year-old in a flash.

"I don't want anybody to feel sorry for me." Alison sniffed. "I want a normal life."

"It—it's not all bad." Becky reached for her cousin's hand. "You can have Shadow back. Now that you're staying in Alberta, you won't have to leave her at Mustang Mountain."

"No. Forget it." Alison straightened her shoulders. "Shadow is your horse."

"But now you won't have to trailer her across the continent," Becky argued. "That's what you were so worried about—that she wouldn't make the long trip ..."

"I said forget it!" Alison insisted. "Shadow hates crowds and noise and traveling. She'll never make a good barrel racing horse."

That wasn't totally true, Alison thought. Her little paint mare was getting better at dealing with strange situations. But my mind is made up, she told herself firmly. I'm not like my father, who breaks promises as if they were breadsticks!

"Anyway," she gulped, "Chuck said he'd help me find a new horse before I went back east. Now that I'm not going back ... we'll have lots of time to horse hunt." Chuck was a cowboy who'd turned up at Mustang Mountain last month. He'd soon be heading home to his ranch near Calgary.

Alison glanced at the note in her hand, then gazed around at the kitchen's warm wood walls. "Mom says she'll pick me up on the weekend. We're moving back into our dumpy little townhouse in Horner Creek," she sighed miserably. "In the middle of summer."

Alison's mother had rented a truck and horse trailer to transport Shadow from the ranch to Horner Creek. The empty trailer bounced in the dust as she and Alison drove down the dirt road from Mustang Mountain two days later.

"Why didn't you tell me you were leaving Shadow behind?" Marion Chant complained. "All this money wasted on a horse van!"

"If you'd bothered to call me, I would have told you," Alison growled. "I'm going to be looking for a new barrel racing horse."

"We can't afford a new horse," Marion announced. "And that's final."

"What about Dad? Doesn't he have to help support me?" Alison asked. Her dad was a wealthy businessman in New York.

"Your father's paying your sister Ashley's college bills." Marion glanced at her daughter's determined face. "Your Grandmother Chant has plenty of money. You could ask her."

"Never!" Alison exploded. "Grandmother hates anything to do with the west, including western riding. You know that. But if I'm going to live in Alberta, I have to barrel race. I need a horse."

"You had a horse." Marion shook her head angrily. "I can't understand why you gave Shadow to Becky—after all the trouble you had adopting the mare in the first place." She glanced in the rearview mirror at the cloud of dust rising behind the horse trailer. "Don't get me wrong—I'm glad I'm not dragging that mustang down this mountain, but why on earth did you give her away?"

"Because I thought we were moving back to New York." Alison could feel her teeth starting to grind. "Remember that plan?"

"Well, then, there's a simple solution." Her mother shrugged. "Get Becky to give Shadow back."

"That may be your simple solution, but it's not mine!" Alison turned away in disgust. The little paint she'd adopted from the wild belonged at Mustang Mountain, not in some Calgary suburb. Becky loved her. And I promised, she reminded herself fiercely.

"Then the matter is closed," Marion told her. "We'll have no more discussion about horses."

Alison looked over her shoulder for one last glimpse of Mustang Mountain disappearing behind the other peaks of the Rockies. Then she hunched down in the front seat of the rental truck and prepared herself not to speak to her mother for the rest of the ride back to Horner Creek.

## CHAPTER 2

# I NEED A HORSE!

"I can't stay in all the time." Alison waved around the living room of the townhouse in Horner Creek. "This place is like a prison." Compared to the rambling ranch house at Mustang Mountain, the townhouse felt narrow and pinched.

"I'm not asking you to." Marion's forehead creased into a frown. "But you have to stop staying out late and running around with kids I don't know."

"If you'd only let me get a horse!" Alison raged. She and her mom had had this argument many times since they moved in a week ago.

"I told you—no more horses. They're far too much trouble and expense. Let's get back to this problem of staying out late at night. I can't be worrying about you every time I go away."

"What do you mean? Where are you going now?" Alison pricked up her ears. This was something new.

Marion lifted her chin. Her smooth dark hair and pale skin mirrored Alison's. "I mean I'm going to be traveling a lot for my job. I'm a professional woman now ..."

"Professional! That's a laugh." Alison spat out the words. "You are professional at messing up my life." She slung her small backpack on one shoulder and jammed her cowboy hat on her head.

"Where do you think you're going?"

"I'm going to a barrel race." Alison headed for the door. "Chuck's picking me up. I'll wait for him outside."

"Who is this Chuck?" Marion demanded.

"I've told you," Alison said over her shoulder, "a guy I met at Mustang Mountain."

"A cowboy!" Marion's voice rose.

"You sound just like Grandmother Chant when you say that," grumbled Alison, knowing how much this insult would hurt. Comparing her mom to Grandmother Chant was like poking her with a hot branding iron. "Yes, Chuck is a cowboy, and he's eighteen."

She strode out the door, hearing her mother call, "Be back by ten-thirty!" No way was she telling her mother Chuck's full name was Charles Rodney Maxwell McClintock and that he was heir to an Alberta fortune. Her mother wouldn't mind her going out with him if she knew Chuck's family ranch, the Bar Q, was one of the largest in the Rocky Mountain foothills.

Let her think I'm running around with a bad crowd, Alison thought savagely. I wish I was!

Waiting for Chuck, she replayed the scene with her mother and twisted in anger. I know I shouldn't talk to Mom that way, she thought. It was mean, comparing her to Grandmother Chant. But she makes me so mad! She says I can't get a horse, as if it's nothing. I have to get a horse, a good barrel racing horse, or I'll go crazy. But she doesn't care about that. She's so totally into her own problems!

The sight of Chuck's dusty dark blue pickup stopped the bitter flow of Alison's thoughts.

"Hey, Chuck." She hopped into the front seat, heaving a sigh at the sight of his hair sticking out from under his hat and the way his freckled cheeks popped out into two round balls when he grinned.

When Chuck McClintock had turned up at Mustang Mountain Ranch, Alison had taken an instant dislike to his red hair and loud laugh. But in the following weeks, she'd learned there was a kind, sensitive person under the rough cowboy mask. If only he wasn't so goofy looking, she might be able to think of him as more than just a friend.

"Morning." Chuck leaned out the driver's-side window and peered at the townhouse. "I thought I might get to meet your mom today."

"She's not here," Alison lied. Actually, she hoped her mother was looking out the front window and feeling upset at the sight of Chuck's dirty truck. That was another thing she didn't like about Chuck. He didn't care how he looked or what he wore. We are complete opposites, Alison sighed again, smoothing down the front of her new painter pants.

"I'm counting on you to help me find a good horse." Alison tried to get her mind off Chuck's looks as he steered down the new suburban street. "I saw some nice-looking horses advertised in *Western Rider*."

"Oh, don't believe those ads." Chuck shook his head. "According to my grandfather, people never tell the truth about a horse they've put up for sale."

"I thought you didn't get along with your grand-father," said Alison. It was the one thing they did have in common—bossy grandparents who held the family purse strings and made everybody dance to their tune. In Chuck's family, it was his Grandfather McClintock—the man who founded Bar Q Ranch. In Alison's family, it was her Grandmother Chant.

"Granddad's a bossy old skinflint, all right." Chuck grinned at her. "But I respect his opinion about horses. He says horse tradin's a crooked business—always has been, always will be." He exaggerated his grandfather's drawl.

"One time, he bought me a horse advertised as 'ready for anything.' That horse was so wild he bucked me into the manure pile. So he bought me another one they said was 'bomb-proof,' and he was half dead and ready for the glue factory."

"Don't talk like that about horses and glue factories!" cried Alison.

"Just a figure of speech," Chuck smiled. "Believe me, if the ad says a horse needs an experienced rider, it means he's a devil. If it says 'needs a good home,' he's ready for the—oops, sorry—ready to be put out to pasture."

He glanced at Alison's stony face. "You might see a good horse at this barrel race we're going to. If you do, you can ask the owner if they want to sell."

"I doubt we'll find a top horse," Alison snorted, "not at this little local show."

The barrel race was at a fairground in a town west of Calgary. In the distance, the mountains stood in a jagged line against the clear blue sky. Horse trailers and trucks littered the fairgrounds, and horses stood patiently tied to them, munching hay.

"What's up with you?" asked Chuck as Alison stalked toward the show ring, her chin in the air. "You're as prickly as a wild rose."

"Nothing ... sorry. I'm mad at my mother. She says I can't get a horse."

Chuck stopped and grabbed her arm. "Wait! Why are we here, then?"

Alison shrugged him off. "I'm still looking for a horse, that's why."

"But …" Chuck's freckles stood out on his puzzled face. Alison felt annoyed just looking at them.

"Listen," she said, "first I'll find the horse, then I'll think of a way to get my mother to buy him. C'mon—you said this was a good place to look." She dragged Chuck toward the ring by the sleeve of his red plaid shirt.

"All right." He laughed. "I'll help, but why does this new horse have to be a him? Can't we look at any mares?"

"No." Alison glanced over her shoulder at Chuck. "I've had two mares, and I lost them both."

The grin left Chuck's face. "Yeah, it's tough, losing a horse."

Alison stopped short. "Oh! Chuck, I'm sorry, I didn't mean … I'm so sorry about Copper." Earlier that summer, Chuck's horse had drowned, swept away in the Cauldron River near Mustang Mountain Ranch. Chuck had never found Copper's body in the fast-flowing water.

"That's okay." Chuck shrugged his broad shoulders. "Like you say, you've lost horses, too."

But not like that! Alison thought. Her beautiful dressage mare, Duchess, had been sold by her father and taken away before she'd had a chance to say good-bye. That was bad enough, but at least she knew Duchess was alive and well looked after. As for Shadow … Alison gulped … the little paint would be much happier with Becky at Mustang Mountain. She shook off these thoughts. "Anyway," she told Chuck, "we're here to find a good horse—let's go look."

They prowled the grounds, watching riders warm up their horses. The barrel racers sat deep in their specially designed saddles, directing their mounts with a single rein. The horses were high-spirited, ready to run.

Alison wished she was in one of those saddles, milling around the starting gate, feeling a powerful horse under her, waiting for her turn.

"See anything you like?" she asked Chuck.

"That tall chestnut looks interesting—the one ridden by the kid in the black hat." Chuck pushed his own cowboy hat back on his head. "Can't tell till you see them run, but he looks nice—"

"I don't want nice," Alison interrupted him. "I want fabulous."

## CHAPTER 3

# SKIPPER'S RUN

Kristy Jones tried to keep Skipper away from the other horses at the gate. He got so excited at the idea of running around those barrels that he could be hard to control.

She didn't notice the dark-haired older girl checking out all the horses, or her red-headed friend. All twelve-year-old Kristy's attention was on her horse. "You have to win today, Skipper," she whispered in the big chestnut's ear. "We have to go home with the jackpot."

She knew she should be focused on having a good run, not on the prize, but it was hard when they needed money so badly. Hard not to remember her father's words, "Sorry, Kris, but I don't know how long we can keep racing Skipper." Between the drought in Alberta and Mad Cow Disease, life on their cattle ranch had been bleak for the past two years. Money was short.

But if Skipper keeps winning, he can pay his own way, Kristy thought.

She remembered the way they'd found Skipper Bug—standing in a field of cows. He was the biggest quarter horse she'd ever seen, a monster over sixteen hands high, and he looked pretty silly hanging with a herd of heifers. But then Kristy learned Skipper was registered, with an impressive set of relatives in the barrel racing business.

Because the owners were anxious to sell, the price was cheap. Kristy and her dad soon found out why. Skipper had zero manners around other horses. Probably from hanging out with cows. Any horse that came too near was likely to get a nip or a kick.

But right from the beginning, he and Kristy had bonded. When they bought him, she was only ten, a scrawny kid with hazel eyes and hair almost the same color as Skipper's chestnut hide. Skipper Bug was six at the time, and two years of training had got him speeding around the barrels—for Kristy. She knew he did it to please her, and no one else. Every time they ran a race, he ran his heart out for her.

This year, they'd been winning. Twenty, thirty, forty dollars at first—enough to pay the gas and entry fees. This race had a jackpot worth nearly a thousand dollars. If they could win!

It was their turn.

Skipper raced through the gate, pounding for the first barrel. He rounded it easily, headed for the second. It tipped and wavered as he cut it close, but stayed up. Now for the third barrel at the top of the ring. Kristy was vaguely aware of people shouting, but her whole focus was on steering a straight line for that barrel, not too close, but close enough to shave seconds off her time.

There! They were around and streaking for the electronic-eye beam at the end of the ring. Now Kristy could hear the cheers. "Go, Kristy, go!"

She leaned forward along Skipper's neck, one hand gripping the horn, the other the rein. She didn't need to spur Skipper or whack him with a cord—he loved this part of the race, heading for the finish line with everything that was in him.

Cheers surrounded them. Kristy let the rein lie loose on Skipper's neck, letting him know it was time to cool down, quit speeding, quit snorting at the other horses and flinging himself around. She rode him out of the ring and away from the horses and riders bunched by the gate. They'd have a second run and the best time would count.

"Time of the last run was fifteen two," the loudspeaker boomed behind her. Kristy stroked Skipper's neck. "Way to go, boy," she whispered. "That was your best time yet!"

Would it be enough to win? She'd have to wait to find out.

In the meantime, there was a slim girl with short dark hair blocking her way. Skipper tossed his head, annoyed at being confronted head on. Kristy slid from her saddle to avoid trouble and took a firm grip on Skipper's bridle.

"I'd like to talk to you," the girl said. "It's about this horse."

"Excuse me." Kristy tried to be polite. "Do you mind getting out of our way? I have to keep Skipper calm—we have a second run."

"It'll only take a minute," the girl insisted. "My name is Alison Chant, and I'm interested in your horse. He is yours, isn't he?"

"Yes, he's mine." Kristy peered at Alison from under the brim of her hat. "But I can't talk now, and Skipper doesn't like strange people getting in his face ..."

This weird girl was going to ruin their second run. Kristy swung Skipper away and hoped the girl wouldn't follow.

CHAPTER 4

# HORSE FOR SALE?

"She wasn't very friendly." Alison climbed the stands to scrunch in beside Chuck. "But the horse looks great up close. You can almost hear his engine running, wanting to race."

"It says here his registered name is Skipper Bug, and the girl's name is Kristy Jones." Chuck pointed to the program. "I think her family's place is near our ranch."

"Skipper Bug?" Alison felt a surge of excitement. "He must be related to Top Skip and Golden Bug. They're famous barrel racing horses." She clutched Chuck's arm. "This could be the one."

"Wait a minute—you can't go buying the first horse you look at." Chuck laughed.

"Why not?" Alison was watching Kristy trying to control the big horse as they circled outside the gate. "Look at him, Chuck! He reminds me of Sunny, the horse Sara Kelly rode in the Calgary Stampede this year—and they won. I rode Sunny, you know," Alison boasted. "It was like riding in my dad's Porsche."

She sat with her elbows on her knees and her chin in her hands, watching the horses race. "That's when I knew I wanted to barrel race," she went on. "I thought I could train Shadow, but she would never love running barrels the way Sunny or this horse Skipper does."

"Wait, don't fall in love," Chuck warned. "Skipper might not be for sale."

Alison ignored him. "You should have seen Sunny at the Stampede," she exulted. "It was the last event of the finals, and Sara rode him like a dream—won fifty thousand dollars, first prize."

"You're thinking big there, kid." Chuck nudged her shoulder. "Listen—Skipper's run is coming up, after they drag the ring. Only one horse has beaten his time so far. This kid Kristy has a chance to win the race."

The tractor with the drag slowly circled the ring, smoothing the churned dirt. The barrels were removed while it did its work, then carefully put back in place. Alison could feel the excitement building. It was almost as if she was getting ready to run herself.

She could see Kristy, a small scrap of a girl on top of that powerful horse, pick up the rein. Skipper leaped forward as if released by a giant spring. They whipped around the first barrel, then the second. Kristy rode a good line for the third, scraped close around it and streaked for home.

"Did you see that?" Alison was on her feet. "Did you see him go?"

"I saw some pretty fine riding!" Chuck hollered over the cheering. "That Kristy Jones knows what she's doing."

"Forget Kristy—what about the horse? Isn't he magnificent?" Alison was staring in awe at Skipper, still circling and stamping in the area near the gate, his shiny coat dark with sweat.

"Time of that run, fourteen nine," the announcer droned. "Kristy Jones and Skipper Bug are now in first place."

Kristy's time held through the last six riders.

"Good going," said Chuck. "She'll take home about a thousand dollars today."

"Let's talk to her again," Alison urged. "She might be friendlier now that she's won."

Kristy was walking Skipper Bug around the trailers when they caught up to her.

"Congratulations!" Alison stuck out her hand. "Like I told you before, I'm Alison Chant, and this is my friend, Chuck McClintock."

Kristy screwed up her small face at Chuck's name, looking more like a ten-year-old than twelve. "McClintock? Your folks got a ranch at Kananaskis?"

"My granddad runs the Bar Q." Chuck nodded. "Your spread is just down the road, isn't it?"

"Yeah, but ours is a pretty small operation." Kristy shrugged. She took off her hat and threw her head back proudly. "We're the Double J, my dad and me and my little sister, Skye."

"I love your horse," Alison butted in. "He has the makings of a real champion."

Kristy patted Skipper Bug's sweaty neck. "Yeah, he ran pretty good for me today." She kept walking. "I have to cool him out now."

"We'll walk with you, if you don't mind," Alison said, keeping pace. "I was wondering if you were interested in selling Skipper."

"Sell my horse?" Kristy stopped dead. Skipper shied and snorted at the sudden change. "No!" She shook her head firmly. "I am not interested in selling him—ever."

"That's fine," said Chuck. He grabbed Alison's hand and started to walk away. "If you don't want to sell, we—"

"Not at any price?" Alison wrenched free of Chuck's hand.

"NO!" Kristy planted her feet like a stubborn horse. "Who wants to buy him—you?" She looked Alison up and down, from her fancy, low-heeled boots to her silver hat band.

"Yes—me. Why?" Alison was taken aback.

"Skipper is way too much horse for you, that's why." Kristy turned Skipper in the other direction.

Alison stood gaping. "How do you know that? I've ridden Sun Glow, the Calgary Stampede champion barrel racing horse."

"That doesn't mean you can ride Skipper." Kristy turned again. Her hazel eyes challenged Alison's dark brown ones. "He doesn't run barrels for anyone but me. So it would be no use you buying him."

"That's ridiculous!" Alison spluttered.

"Alison, she knows her horse," Chuck rumbled in her ear. "Let's go."

"I can't believe she doesn't think I could ride this horse," Alison hissed back. "I've ridden every kind of horse, including high-strung jumpers. I could handle this horse with one hand."

Kristy glared at her. "Is that so? Would you like to try?"

"What do you mean?"

"I mean, there's a break now before the pole bending event. They're letting the horses warm up in the ring. You can ride Skipper, right now, if you think you can manage him."

This was a deliberate dare. "Hold this!" Alison thrust her backpack at Chuck. "I'm going for a ride."

"I'd better lead him to the ring." Kristy waved her off. "It's not safe to ride him out here in public. Too many people milling around."

She's exaggerating, thought Alison. Look at Skipper walking along beside us. He's a big sweetie. Chuck was tugging at her shirt. "Leave me alone." She squirmed away. "I know what I'm doing."

"All right." Chuck sighed. "I'll be in the stands watching."

But as soon as she swung into the saddle, Alison could feel the ripple of protest that swept from Skipper's flattened ears to his clamped golden tail. This was not Kristy—this was a stranger on his back. He snorted and charged across the ring.

"Easy, whoa!" Alison hauled on the rein and instantly knew she'd made a big mistake. Skipper spun in a circle, as only a good quarter horse can do, so fast she had no time to react. Before she knew it, she was slipping sideways, out of the saddle. Her slippery cotton pants speeded the slide.

I'm falling! Alison had time to realize, then the crepe sole of her new boot got stuck in the stirrup. She was hanging off Skipper's right side, grasping for the saddle, his mane, anything to pull herself up.

Things happened in slow motion. Skipper turned his head and fixed her with a wild white-rimmed eye, then took off, bouncing her through the dirt.

Alison heard pounding hooves behind her. Skipper Bug jolted to a stop. She looked into a pair of worried blue eyes, recognized the shirt and neck scarf of one of the top riders. Another rider held Skipper's rein.

"Th-thanks," she stammered to the young woman who pulled her upright and pried her boot free from the twisted stirrup.

"You okay?" The girl looked rattled and disapproving. "Good thing Diane and I were close, you could have been dragged to death."

"I know. Thanks." Alison slid off onto shaky legs. She felt like there was a blaze of bright neon lights flashing "IDIOT" all around her, and everyone was watching.

"I'll be okay now," she told the woman.

Kristy ran up to them, a lead rope in her hand, a frightened look on her face.

"You set me up!" Alison hissed furiously as Kristy snapped the lead onto Skipper's bridle.

"No, I didn't." The twelve-year-old glared at her. "I told you Skipper was too much for you."

"She sure did!" Chuck's face was red from rushing from the stands. "That was ugly to watch." He led Alison away from the milling horses and the onlookers' stares. "That girl knew exactly what the horse would do. You were lucky. You could have been really hurt."

"It was my dumb clothes." Alison brushed herself off as they headed for his truck. "I could have handled Skipper if my pants weren't so slippery and my boot hadn't got stuck."

"You're crazy." Chuck shook his head. "It was the horse, not your clothes. Don't tell me you still want to buy Skipper?"

"I'm not sure." Alison was dazed from her near disaster. The nasty look in Skipper's eye haunted her. "He has some bad habits—but I'd like to look at him again."

"He's not for sale."

"My father says everything's for sale—for a price." Alison tipped up her chin.

Chuck raised one eyebrow. "So? From what you've told me about your father, you don't need his advice."

Alison was silent. Why did Chuck always zero in on the truth? She definitely didn't want to be like her dad. But she might want that horse.

Kristy watched Alison walk away and noted with satisfaction how she leaned on Chuck and limped a little. "I guess we fixed her, didn't we?" She stroked Skipper's glossy neck. "Miss Hot Stuff! I hope we've seen the end of her."

She walked Skipper back to the trailer, where her father was waiting. Mike Jones was a short man with thinning gray hair and sharp features. He shook his head as Kristy approached.

"I saw that," he scolded. "What did you think you were doin', letting that girl ride Skipper?"

"Pop, she wanted to buy him!" The words poured out of Kristy. "I told her he was too much horse for her, but she wouldn't believe me."

"So you thought you'd show her ..." Mike rubbed his chin. "You put us all at risk. What would have happened if that girl had got hurt?"

Kristy bit her lip.

"Or what if Skipper got away from her and ran himself into one of those steel barriers?" her father went on. "If you're goin' to keep racing him, you're goin' to have to never pull a stunt like that again."

"I'm sorry," Kristy murmured. "But, Pop, she was so pushy."

"And you lost your temper, which never works where horses are concerned. As if you didn't know that." Mike put his arm around Kristy. "I know it won't happen again, girl."

Kristy let go of a big breath. That snooty girl had almost ruined this day for them.

"We won the jackpot, Pop." Kristy pulled the envelope out of her pocket. "A thousand bucks!"

"It's welcome, Kris." He smiled at her. "Now let's get that big fellow unsaddled and brushed down. And don't worry—Skipper's not for sale."

CHAPTER 5

# THE BAR Q RANCH

As the sun set over the suburban street, Chuck dropped Alison off at her townhouse, and she watched his truck drive away.

She went slowly up the steps, turned the key in the lock and braced herself for an argument with her mother as she walked through the door.

But the house was empty.

A note on the kitchen counter said her mother had gone shopping. "Back soon, Love Mom," the note ended. Alison crumpled it in her hand.

"I miss Becky," Alison groaned out loud, collapsing on the couch. She'd had only two conversations with Becky since she'd moved, both on that crackly Mustang

Mountain radio-phone, where you could hardly hear what a person was saying!

If only her cousin had wanted to live with them in Horner Creek, like she did until this summer, she wouldn't be so lonely. Alison could picture Becky's flushed face as she announced her decision to stay at the wilderness ranch. "I'm sorry, but I want to stay here. I can finish school by correspondence, and Mom really needs me, and I can train Shadow ..."

These were only excuses, Alison knew.

The real truth was that Becky was sick of putting up with the Chant family. She'd lived with them in New York for a year and a half while she went to school. But Marion and Roger Chant fought bitterly the whole time. When they finally separated, Becky moved with Alison and her mother to Horner Creek, where she had to listen to Alison and her mother battle like two tiger sharks in a tank. In both houses, the air had been thick with misery—loud, horrible fights and long, cold silences.

We Chants are no fun to live with, Alison admitted to herself. She felt faintly guilty, as though somehow it was all her fault.

She stood up and went to look at herself in the mirror. Her new shirt was grubby and her pants creased and dirty from being dragged through the dirt. Mom would have a fit if she knew I sat on the couch in my riding clothes, Alison thought—not that I stayed on Skipper Bug very long!

The humiliation of that fall came back as she stared at her image. She'd always been proud of herself as a rider—now that pride was disappearing.

"I don't know who you are," she told her reflection in the mirror. "You don't even have a horse!"

"Can you come out to the ranch?" Chuck called to say the next morning. "I might have a solution to your horse problem."

He sounded mysterious.

"What is it?" Alison begged. "Did you buy a new horse?"

"Wait and see," he chuckled. "I'll pick you up at two."

"Chuck again?" Marion said when she heard Alison's news. "You're seeing a lot of that boy. I want to meet him."

Alison gave her most annoying shrug. "Sure. Someday."

Her mother didn't have to worry, Alison thought. She wasn't in the least attracted to Chuck. She wondered why. Maybe because he was so large and solid, instead of slim like Becky's boyfriend, Rob, or slight and wiry, like Meg's friend Thomas. Chuck was nice enough, but too much of a hulk for her.

She thought about that again when he came to the door that afternoon. Definitely a hulk—tall, with broad shoulders and a thick neck. Not my type, Alison sighed to herself.

"Your mom's not here again?" Chuck peered around the living room.

"No, she's at work." Alison reached for her hat in the hall closet. "She's a 'professional woman' these days, she says."

"What does she do?" Chuck asked as Alison locked the door behind them.

"Not sure, exactly. Something in sales. Ski clothes and stuff like that," Alison called over her shoulder as she ran down the steps to the truck. "Why are you so interested in my mother?"

Chuck pushed his hat up. "Just trying to find out what makes you tick."

"Well, that's easy. I hate my parents and my life. I have no control over anything. I can't make friends or get involved in anything at school because the next day I might be living in Timbuktu!" Alison slid into the pickup's front seat. "Ugh. Look at the dust. Don't you ever clean this truck?"

Chuck ignored this remark. "Don't worry. Your life is about to get better."

"With this mystery horse of yours?"

"Just wait, you'll see."

The Bar Q stretched far over the rolling hills of Kananaskis Country, west of Horner Creek. The ranch buildings were sheltered in a broad valley, tucked out of sight from the road. White fence stretched as far as the eye could see. Even for Alison, used to the beauty of the foothills country, it was breathtakingly lovely.

"Well, this is it." Chuck brought the truck to a stop in front of the ranch house. "The home spread."

Alison heard the bitterness in his voice. Was there something wrong in this dream house, too?

"You'll have to meet my grandfather, later." Chuck stepped out of the truck. "First I want to show you something."

He led the way to a paddock behind the long, low barn. A horse stood on the other side of the fence, facing them. The horse had the black mane and tail of a bay, with four black stockings and a dark brown coat. His body was narrow and his head enormous.

"That's the horse?" Alison gasped. "That slab-sided bay?"

"I call him Lucky Ralph because he has a white patch on his forehead in the shape of a lucky clover." Chuck leaned on a fence rail. "And I bought him from a cowboy named Ralph who was going to lose him in a poker game."

Alison shuddered. "This clunker is supposed to be the solution to my problems?"

"Just because Ralph was going to gamble this horse away doesn't mean he's good for nothing." Chuck whistled, and the bay ambled toward them. "Ralph was flat broke and desperate—I caught him at a weak moment."

Lucky Ralph had reached the fence and stretched out his neck to see if Chuck had a treat. "I admit he's a bit thin at the moment," said Chuck, "but he'll fill out when he gets some good feed in him."

"A bit thin?" Alison looked doubtfully at the bay. "He's the ugliest horse I've ever seen. Look at his head! It's way too big for his body."

"Beauty isn't everything," Chuck muttered.

"What makes you think he'd be any good as a barrel racing horse?"

"Ralph bought him off the quarter horse race track." Chuck reached in his pocket for a horse treat. "He was a great sprinter, but they rode him too hard. He lost his wind, and his will to run. And maybe he just got bored running in a straight line." Chuck held out the treat to Lucky Ralph, and the horse gently nibbled it off his hand. "See, he's got a nice personality. I call him Lucky, for short."

Alison sighed. "Sorry, Chuck, but I don't want a makeover project. I want a horse like Skipper or Sunny— a winner."

"You won't find a horse like that in a hurry." Chuck looked down at her.

"But that's what I want," Alison said stubbornly. "What's the use of barrel racing if I can't be the best?"

Chuck stared at the slender girl with her hands on her hips and her shoulders thrown back. He'd seen that proud, determined look on Alison's face before. "I guess you're kind of used to buying the best of everything," he said slowly, "but some things you can't buy—you've got to work for them."

"I don't intend to train a broken-down racehorse. I'm starting at the top. If you don't want to help, don't." Alison turned her back on Chuck and stalked away.

"Well, big guy, she put you in your place." Chuck rubbed the clover-shaped star on Lucky's forehead. "Don't feel bad, she's done it to me already."

He followed Alison toward the house. "I'll help," Chuck promised. "Let's go horse hunting at the next barrel race—this Saturday at Wilton."

"That's better." Alison smiled up at him. "Look, I didn't mean to dump on poor old Lucky, it's just ..."

"We get the picture." Chuck grinned. "Now, come and meet the old man."

"Your father?" Chuck hadn't told her much about his family—just that he was an only child, and his parents were divorced.

"No, Dad's off making money in oil. My grandfather." His eyes narrowed.

Alison remembered he'd said the old man was a tyrant who bossed the whole family around. She squared her shoulders. Bossy old tyrants were something she knew all about.

She'd expected the house to be dark inside and full of heavy old furniture. Instead, it was flooded with sunshine from floor-to-ceiling windows that looked over the mountains like a ship's prow. The living room ceiling was two stories high, roofed with polished log beams, and the walls and floor were the same polished pine.

A stone fireplace covered one wall, and in front of it

stood a man with silver hair. He was tall and lean, but a little stooped, and his eyes had the look of an eagle ready to swoop on its prey.

Alison strode forward with her hand outstretched. "Good afternoon, sir. I'm Alison Chant."

The steely eyes twinkled under bushy gray brows. "So, you're the girl who's keepin' my grandson here, instead of where I want him—at McGill University in Montreal."

Alison's eyebrows shot up. How could the old man think she was responsible for Chuck not wanting to go to McGill?

Old Mr. McClintock sized her up. "I can see his point, although you look too young for him. I'm Walter McClintock, his grandfather."

"Yes, sir," said Alison. "Chuck's told me about you, too."

This brought a gust of laughter from the old man. "I'll bet he has. I understand your family is from the east. I lived in the east myself as a student, many years ago. Three generations of McClintocks have graduated from McGill. Chuck will be the fourth—he and my other grandson, Craig McClintock." He motioned with his hand. "Craig! Where are you hidin'? Come over here."

"Hi." Alison heard a voice from the far corner of the room. She spun around and saw a boy rising from the depths of a leather armchair that was facing the mountains.

Alison felt her heart race as he walked toward them. Craig looked nothing like his cousin Chuck!

# CHAPTER 6

# COUSIN CRAIG

He was gorgeous.

Craig McClintock had long, long legs and a cowboy's confident stride. Alison took in the silver buckle at his waist, the dark, wavy hair that curled adorably around his ears. As he walked toward her with the light behind him, her boy radar flashed hot! hot! hot!

"Of course, Craig's only sixteen—he has another year of high school before he heads off to college," his grandfather was saying. "He's my son William's boy. Doesn't look much like Chuck, does he?"

"Uh … no," Alison stammered. "Cousins don't always … look the same. My cousin Becky and I don't look anything alike, do we, Chuck?" She glanced at Chuck and saw him frowning at her. She felt herself blush—was her reaction to Craig that obvious?

"Howdy, Craig." Chuck turned to his cousin. "I didn't know you were coming out to the ranch today."

"I didn't either." Craig looked steadily back at Chuck. "Had a special request from Granddad to come."

"I thought since we were havin' a young lady visit, she might as well take a look at all the young men around the place," Grandfather McClintock drawled.

Suddenly, Alison was furious with the old man. He wanted Chuck to leave the ranch for college, so he was setting her up with the younger grandson—someone more suitable—the way he'd breed horses! How dare he?

I don't care how good-looking Craig is, she thought fiercely. I'm not going to play this game.

"Nice to meet you, Craig." She focused her eyes over his head at the mountain view. No more butterflies in the stomach and racing heart for her!

"Was Chuck showing you that knock-kneed nag of his?" Craig laughed. "He's got great plans for that horse."

Alison realized at that moment that Chuck had been willing to give up something he cared about for her. She said loyally, "Lucky seems like a nice horse. Just because he's not beautiful doesn't mean he can't run."

She saw Chuck's whole face lift, from his eyebrows to the corners of his mouth. He took a step closer to Alison. "Yeah. Beauty isn't everything. Sea Biscuit was one of the best racehorses in history, and he was plug ugly."

Alison shot a look at old Mr. McClintock. His hawk's eyes were flashing from one face to another. "Craig," he said, "why don't you show young Alison here around the place?"

Craig looked surprised at this sudden suggestion, but he smiled politely. "Would you like to?"

His smile could melt a glacier, Alison thought. She'd have to be especially careful not to look at him when he smiled!

"Maybe another time," she gulped. "I have to ask Chuck to take me home right now. My mom will be worried if I'm not home soon. And please don't worry, Mr. McClintock, I'm too young to be serious about boys, like you say. Chuck and I are just good friends, aren't we, Chuck?"

He was beaming at her now, his freckles popping. "That's right. Anyway, as you can see, Granddad, Alison's much too smart to be interested in a clod like me. Did I tell you how she found my watch and figured out I wasn't the poor cowboy I pretended to be?"

When they were at Mustang Mountain Ranch in July, Alison had found Chuck's seven thousand dollar Rolex watch in his jeans pocket while washing his clothes. She'd also recognized the label in his top-quality shirt and his expensive socks.

"Why would you pretend ... ?" Craig looked puzzled.

"Because being a McClintock can leave a bad taste in the mouth," Chuck said slowly. He glared at his grandfather. "Let's go, Alison."

Alison shared a grin with him as they strode out of the lofty room. Sometimes, she thought, Chuck isn't as goofy as I think.

"Look," Chuck said as they sped back to Horner Creek, "Craig's really a decent guy. It wasn't his fault—Granddad plays with all of us like poker chips."

"I know. I've told you about my Grandmother Chant. She tries the same stuff. That's really why my mom and dad broke up. My grandmother just got it into her head that Mom wasn't good enough for the fabulous Chant family. My mother spent years trying to measure up, but it never worked."

"Same with my folks." Chuck sighed. "My mother couldn't take being bossed around by the old man. I can't, either. But, hey! I loved the way you stood up to him."

"I wonder what makes them do it?" Alison said, still thinking about her grandmother. "I mean, they make so many people unhappy—two whole generations of people!"

"Let's not think about them." Chuck grinned at her. "Barrel racing on the weekend? Look at some more horses?"

"Sure." Alison nodded. "Speaking of horses, I'm sorry about Lucky ... he just isn't my kind of ..."

"No problem," Chuck laughed. "I feel lucky enough for both of us. You called me your good friend in there."

Alison felt herself blush. "Don't make too much of that," she warned.

At the Double J Ranch, Kristy Jones stuffed an armload of hay into Skipper's hay net.

She watched him munching and sighed. "This hay is so expensive, you'll have to win big this fall to buy you enough to get through the winter."

Skipper Bug lifted his head and whickered at the sound of Kristy's voice. He liked to hold up his end of a conversation.

"Our hay crop was pathetic," Kristy went on. "We'll have to buy most of what you need." She cut the twine around a new bale with a knife and lifted off a large, fragrant flake. "And you need the best feed to help you run fast, don't you, big guy?"

Skipper blew a happy horse sound. He was content when Kristy was in the barn, and his ears followed the sound of her voice as she headed down the center aisle with her empty wheelbarrow.

"A couple more chores, and we'll go for a practice run," she called over her shoulder.

Just then, Kristy's little sister, Skye, came running toward her.

"Kristy, come quick! Something's wrong with Pop!"

Kristy dropped the wheelbarrow and tore after her sister to the house. Inside, she found her father collapsed in a kitchen chair, his face the color of stove ash.

"Get me my pills ... from the bathroom," Mike gasped.

Kristy flew up the stairs. She fumbled among the things in her dad's bathroom drawer, grabbed the bottle of pills and dashed back to the kitchen.

"I've got them, Dad." She quickly ran a cup of water from the tap and hurried to his side. "Can you take this, or do you need me to help?"

She held out the small white pill to her father. He waved away the water but seized the pill and chewed it carefully. In a few seconds, color came back to his face. She could see he was breathing more easily.

"Come and lie down," Kristy said. She helped him into the shabby living room and settled him on the couch. "I'll make you some tea."

It was then she noticed her sister's frightened face in the living room doorway. Skye was only seven. If Kristy was a scrap of a girl, Skye was half a scrap, tiny and thin, with big eyes and a small pointed chin, like a kitten.

"I was so sc-scared." Skye's voice trembled. "I didn't know whether to stay with Pop or run to get you." Tears trickled down her cheeks.

"You did fine." Kristy gave her a hug and smoothed Skye's brown hair back off her cheeks. "Pop's feeling better. The doctor says he'll be all right if he takes his pills when he gets one of these spells. I'll show you where he keeps them so that next time, you can get them yourself, okay?"

"O-kay," Skye sobbed. "I wish Mom was here."

"Shhh! So do I, but we don't talk about that in front of Pop." Kristy led her little sister to the kitchen table and handed her the cup of water. Their mother hadn't been able to take the drought and the failing cattle business. As the land dried out, she seemed to dry out, too. Finally, she'd packed her bags and left for Edmonton. "You'll be all right with your dad." Marta Jones had smoothed Kristy's auburn hair. "You both love horses and this godforsaken ranch. But I'll send for Skye as soon as I get settled. I don't want her to grow up here."

That had been six months ago, and she hadn't sent for Skye yet. Kristy hoped she wouldn't. If the rains came, and Mad Cow Disease went away, maybe her mom would come back.

"I don't want this—it was Pop's water." Skye shoved the cup away.

Kristy took the cup and poured it out in the sink. As she ran tap water into a clean glass, she thought, if Mom knew how sick Pop was, I'm sure she'd come back. But he doesn't want me to tell. And what if he's right? What if she didn't come even then?

She walked back to the table and handed the glass to Skye. "Who will help me trailer Skipper to the races on the weekend?" she said out loud. "Pop won't be able to do it."

"Why do you have to go and barrel race, anyway?"

"Because we paid lots of money for Skipper's entry fee. And he's got to win! It's more important than ever."

## CHAPTER 7

# READY TO RACE

Alison couldn't get Craig McClintock off her mind.

She felt she was being disloyal to Chuck in some way, thinking so much about his cousin. But in the days that followed her visit to the Bar Q Ranch, Craig's face kept swimming up from her memory and stopping her in the middle of whatever she was doing. She saw him with the light behind him, coming toward her. Saw his fine features and wavy hair. Felt her heart race all over again when their eyes met.

"Grow up," she told herself at one point. "You've been getting crushes on guys since you were twelve, and they never last—you know that! Remember Jesse, the cowhand at Mustang Mountain the first year you were there? Or Chance, the dark mysterious stranger who rode in the second year? You had a crush on him, and he turned out to be a horrible bounty hunter."

But no matter how much she scolded herself, the memory of Craig's face scorched through all the layers of common sense. Why couldn't Chuck have dark wavy hair and smooth skin and a slim, athletic build like his cousin?

"Craig's probably a spoiled brat," she tried to convince herself, but she didn't believe it. He had been as embarrassed by his grandfather's trying to pair them off as she had. She wished she could see him again and tell him she knew it wasn't his fault.

"Listen to yourself!" Alison paced the floor. "Now you're dreaming up reasons to see Craig again. You're never going to see him again, and that's final." So why did she arrange her Cheerios to spell "CM" or look up "McClintock" in the telephone book to see if she could find out where Craig lived?

It was useless, anyway—there were dozens of McClintocks in the Calgary area!

"Okay if I pick you up at eight tomorrow morning?" Chuck called to ask on Friday.

"Why so early?"

"Well, the barrel races start at ten." Chuck's deep voice rumbled on the other end of the phone. "And I want to cruise by and pick up Craig on our way out to Wilton."

"Craig?" Alison heard herself squeak. "Your cousin, Craig?" So much for never seeing Craig again.

"Yeah, he's coming with us. That's okay, isn't it?"

Alison found it hard to breathe. "Uh—sure, that'll be fine." She tried to sound completely uninterested.

"Because if it's not okay for some reason, you can tell me," said Chuck.

"It's great. See you at eight," Alison choked and hung up the phone.

She couldn't help it. She dressed and undressed five times Saturday morning.

First outfit—too ordinary.

Second outfit—too flashy.

Third outfit—too obviously meant to impress Craig.

Fourth outfit—too drab.

Finally, she was out of time and had to throw on whatever she picked up first. A blue plaid shirt and dark jeans. The doorbell rang and there was Chuck, beaming, freckle-faced, on her doorstep.

"Wow!" He whistled. "You look great!"

Alison couldn't return his grin. To cover her flustered feelings, she blurted, "Come and meet my mother."

"Sure." Chuck plowed through the doorway, raising his hat.

Leave it on! Alison wanted to shout at him. His hair

looked so much worse without his hat—flat on top and sticking straight out over his ears.

Sure enough, her mother gasped at the sight of so much red hair and so much Chuck. He seemed to fill the tiny townhouse kitchen.

"Pleased to meet you, Mrs. Chant," he boomed. "Alison sure does take after you. You look just like her!"

Alison wanted to sink through the floor. Her mother was staring at Chuck as if a large foreign body had invaded her tidy universe.

"You'll have to excuse me," Marion said. "Alison didn't tell me I was going to meet you this morning."

"That was my fault." Chuck grinned his wide cheek-bunching grin. "I've been pestering her to introduce me ever since you moved in. It doesn't seem right that Alison and I are hanging out together without you and I ever laying eyes on each other."

Marion sniffed. She glanced at Chuck's dusty cowboy boots and the tracks they made on her clean kitchen floor. Alison knew her mother was about to say something rude to Chuck. She might not let her go to the barrel race with him.

"Mother," she shot in quickly, "Chuck's family owns an enormous ranch in Kananaskis. His father's in oil."

Her mother's face relaxed. "Is that so?"

"I'm afraid it is." Chuck nodded. "Well, we'd better be going. That is, if I have your permission to take Alison to the barrel races in Wilton today? I'll have her home good and early."

"Alison doesn't wait for permission to do what she wants," Marion said. "But I appreciate your asking."

She looks stunned, Alison thought. As if a rambunctious puppy has just transformed itself into a show dog before her eyes. Chuck's old-fashioned manners had won her over—that, plus the hint he was rich.

"Your mom doesn't seem so bad," Chuck muttered as he put the pickup in gear.

"Yeah." Alison sighed. "She's all right, sometimes."

"I'm sure she's going through a bad time right now," Chuck said soothingly.

"A bad time that's lasted fifteen years!" Alison exclaimed. It was true. She couldn't remember a time when her mother wasn't in some kind of crisis.

"Anyway, she's pretty—like you." He glanced at her. "You look different today, somehow."

I wish he hadn't noticed, Alison thought. She knew perfectly well she looked different because she was excited about seeing Craig.

"Alison? You okay?"

"Sure." She forced her thoughts away from Craig. "I hope Kristy and Skipper Bug will be at Wilton," she said. "I can't wait to see that horse run again." She thought about the big chestnut powering around the barrels with the slender girl hugged close to his back, almost as if she were part of the horse. She shook away the picture of their closeness. Skipper Bug should belong to her, not Kristy Jones.

Out at the Double J Ranch, Kristy loaded Skipper Bug into the back of the trailer belonging to Melissa Dale's family. The two girls had been rival barrel racers ever since they'd got into the sport as nine-year-olds.

"It's nice of your family to take us to Wilton." Kristy closed the trailer door. She hated to ask for help.

"That's okay." Melissa smiled. "You'd do the same for me if my dad was sick."

Kristy glanced at her house's sagging front porch, where Skye was standing by her dad's chair, waving good-bye. Sure, they'd do the same, if her dad ever made it out of that chair. A chill crept round her heart. What would they do if he didn't get better? What would happen to her, and Skye, and the ranch? The Double J was falling apart, but Kristy loved this place with a passion that filled her whole twelve-year-old body.

"We have to win today," she whispered to herself as she climbed into the Dales' truck.

## CHAPTER 8

# KRISTY'S LOSS

Craig lived in an older section of Calgary near the Elbow River. Trees grew tall along the winding streets.

Chuck honked his horn as they turned into Craig's driveway.

"Chuck, that's so rude!" cried Alison. Then Craig came striding toward the truck, and all she could think was that he was even better-looking than she remembered. He opened the door next to her.

"Squeeze over."

Craig hopped into the front seat beside her. Soon they were rolling down the quiet street, with Alison squeezed tight between the two boys. She felt dizzy, having Craig next to her. "Why—what made you want to come to the barrel races?" she managed to splutter.

"Oh, I don't know." Craig shrugged. "Chuck mentioned you were going, and I didn't have anything else to do."

Alison noticed how sweetly his hair curled along the back of his neck. "So, are you a big barrel racing fan?" she asked, just to keep talking.

"Nah, I always thought it was kind of a girl thing," admitted Craig.

"Lots of guys barrel race, too!" Alison straightened her shoulders. "Maybe not at the Calgary Stampede, but ... other places."

He turned to smile at her and she almost melted into the seat. "That's what Chuck says, too."

"I told him he'd have a good time watching the races." Chuck nodded. "Lots of pretty girls—pretty horses, too. Alison's looking at one called Skipper Bug, a big, fast horse with a lot of power."

"You planning to buy him?" Craig smiled again.

"If I can." Alison swallowed hard. "The trouble is, he's not really for sale."

"Will Skipper Bug be racing?" Craig asked.

"I hope so!" cried Alison. "I can't wait to see him run the barrels and win again." She felt bubbles of excitement fizzing up inside. Part of it was sitting next to Craig. Part was thinking that big beautiful horse—that champion horse—might soon be hers.

As soon as Kristy unloaded Skipper from the Dales' trailer, she knew he was having an off day. Skipper stumbled coming down the ramp and seemed grumpy being tied to a strange trailer. He tossed his head at Melissa's horse, Samarkand, and tried to nip his neck.

"Stop that!" Kristy ordered. "I'm sorry," she apologized to Melissa. "He has terrible manners."

"Do you need help, Kristy?" Melissa's mother looked nervously from Skipper Bug to the small girl struggling to control him.

"No, we'll be fine, Mrs. Dale." Kristy took a firm grip on Skipper's lead shank. "I'll warm him up away from the other horses."

Kristy quickly tacked up Skipper and led him to a quieter section of the grounds. It didn't help that she had butterflies dancing in her stomach—Skipper was aware of every bit of tension in her body. "It's just one race," she told herself. "There'll be lots more."

But she didn't believe it. She needed to win today. And she wasn't fooling Skipper. He stamped and reared as she tightened the cinch. "Come on, boy," Kristy urged. "Just stand still and let me get you ready to run."

It was even worse once she was on Skipper's back. He shied at every strange sound. It took all her skill to keep him from charging in among the crowd of horses and people around the gate to the ring.

"We're going to be fine, we're going to be fine," Kristy kept telling the big chestnut, leaning forward to pat his neck under his reddish gold mane. "You just do your job and win this race for us. Win some money for the ranch."

They did win the junior division, beating Melissa and Samarkand. Now for the sweepstakes race, where all the divisional winners competed for the top prize—the jackpot!

Circling, turning, backing up, Kristy tried everything to keep Skipper's mind so busy he didn't have time to worry about the other horses milling around the gate. Each horse would run twice, and their best time would automatically count.

This was their first run. They had to wait for the tractor to drag the ring and two other horses to run, but finally, it was their turn.

Kristy had Skipper in the alley, focused and ready for takeoff. She lifted the rein. At this signal, Skipper took off like a rocket from a launching pad, speeding for the first barrel.

Kristy barely heard the announcement ringing over the public address system. "Sorry—you'll have to start again. The electronic eye malfunctioned."

The electronic-eye beam they crossed at the start gate, the trigger for the clock to time their race, had failed.

Disaster! Skipper was already leaning into his first turn. Thrown off balance by Kristy's sudden loss of concentration, he stumbled into the barrel. Kristy fought for control as it rattled around his legs.

"Kristy Jones—please go back and start your run again," the loudspeaker blared.

Kristy shook her head violently. No. No use to do this first run over. It would take too long to get Skipper calm enough to start the pattern again. He didn't understand electronic eyes. All he knew was that the sequence of turns 'he'd learned was broken, and all the pent-up energy to dash around the barrels and race for home was stalled.

This was awful! Kristy fought to control half a ton of confused horse, get him out of the ring and away from the muddle at the gate—back to an open space where he could walk and jog off all that frustration.

"We'll get another run," she soothed. "Every horse gets two tries. Next time, nothing will go wrong." She hoped she was right. For a calmer horse, a false start wouldn't matter. For Skipper, it was enough to ruin his day. If she was lucky, she'd get him ready for the second run in time. At that moment, she glimpsed Alison, her eyebrows drawn together in an angry frown, striding toward her. The big red-headed guy and another boy lagged sheepishly behind.

"That's all we need," Kristy muttered. "That weird girl."

She circled Skipper away from Alison, but her voice rang high and clear behind them. "That stupid electronic eye. They should make sure those things work before they start the race!"

Skipper Bug snorted and bobbed his head. With his horse's almost 360-degree vision, he could see Alison—and he remembered her from their last ride.

Alison glared at Kristy, hands on hips. "Aren't you going to lodge a protest or anything?"

Who did this girl think she was? Kristy leaned over her saddle horn and smoothed Skipper's mane. "I'm trying to get Skipper ready for his next run in a few minutes," she said. "Could you get out of our way?"

Leaving Alison spluttering in the dust, she rode Skipper toward the gate. They were announcing her second run, coming up after the next drag.

Skipper stamped and charged in the alley until it was finally time to take off. They made a fast start, zipping right around the first barrel, left around the second. Then a good clean run for the third, at the top of the arena. They were cutting it close, shaving seconds.

Too close! The barrel wobbled and fell as they raced for the finish line.

Kristy heard the crowd's loud groans. A fallen barrel was an automatic penalty of five seconds. Enough to lose the race, no matter how fast Skipper had run.

Kristy reined him in so he wasn't running flat out at the end. No use risking anything now. They'd lost the sweepstakes and the prize money.

The whole day was a waste. Her divisional prize would cover the entry fee and expenses, that was all.

"I'm sorry," she murmured to Mrs. Dale back at the trailer. "You brought us all this way for nothing." Tears of disappointment stung her eyes.

"It's all right, dear." Mrs. Dale was loading equipment into the trailer. "You can't win every race."

Kristy reached up to remove Skipper's bridle. "But we have to ..." she whispered, slipping on his halter. She led him away from the bustle around the trailers to cool him off.

Then, coming around a large horse van, she saw Alison again, heading straight for them. "You should lodge a protest," she was saying. "It's their fault Skipper lost!"

"What business is it of yours?" Kristy met her with a blazing face. She kept a firm hand on Skipper's lead.

"It's my business because I want to buy him," Alison announced. "I'll pay you twenty thousand dollars."

Kristy gaped at the older girl. That was a heap of money! Enough to keep the ranch going for a long time. How long would it take her to earn twenty thousand dollars in barrel racing jackpots? Too long, especially if they kept losing like today.

She took a firmer grip on Skipper Bug. She couldn't let him go!

## CHAPTER 9

# ALISON'S OFFER

"Well?" Alison challenged. "What do you say?" Inwardly, she was shivering at her own nerve. She didn't have twenty thousand dollars, or anything close to that. What would she do if Kristy said yes?

"I'll have to ask my dad ..." Kristy mumbled.

"Is he here?" Alison looked around.

"No, he had to ... stay home," said Kristy. "Do you have a telephone number where we can call you?"

Alison stared at her. Was her father really at home? Was Kristy telling the truth, or stalling? "Sure, I'll write down my number." She took a notebook out of her backpack, ripped off a page, scribbled her phone number and handed it to Kristy.

Kristy stuffed the paper in her pocket without even

looking at it. "We'll think it over," she muttered, leading Skipper away.

Alison watched them go. "What a horse," she breathed. She could see Skipper's ears relax as Kristy led him to an open space. He was even more beautiful when he was relaxed than when he was running barrels.

Craig and Chuck came strolling up behind her. "What did she say?" Chuck wanted to know.

Alison sighed. "She said she'd think about selling him."

"He's way too much horse for you." Chuck shook his shaggy head. "I was watching Kristy in there. She has trouble managing Skipper and she's been riding him for years."

"She's just a kid." Alison threw back her head. "I wouldn't have any trouble riding him once I showed him who's boss."

Craig laughed. "Are you always so sure of yourself?"

"When I'm right!" Alison could feel a blush creeping up her cheeks.

"And sometimes even when you're wrong," Chuck grumbled under his breath.

Alison shot him a look. She wished he hadn't got to know her so well up at Mustang Mountain.

"I saw you talking to that girl Alison Chant," Melissa said as she helped Kristy load Skipper Bug in the trailer for the trip home.

"Do you know her?" Kristy stopped in her tracks.

"Sure. She's a friend of Sara Kelly's. She lives in Horner Creek."

"Is Alison a barrel racer?" asked Kristy.

"She rode in a few races this spring. She has a neat little mustang paint mare."

"Then why does she want my horse?" Kristy stared at Melissa. "She just offered to buy Skipper for twenty thousand dollars."

"Whew!" Melissa whistled. "Well, she can afford it. Her family's rich, I hear."

So it's true! Kristy thought as she settled Skipper in the trailer. Alison wasn't kidding. She has the money and she really wants to buy him.

She would have to talk to her dad. But in her heart, Kristy knew what he'd say. Horses, no matter how special, could always be replaced. The ranch couldn't.

The phone rang at Horner Creek the following Monday afternoon.

"This is Kristy Jones."

Alison sucked in a deep breath. "Hi."

"My dad and I have decided to sell Skipper to you." Kristy's voice was low and hoarse. "For twenty thousand, like you said."

"That's—great." Alison swallowed hard, wishing she hadn't offered so much.

"There's, uh, just one thing," Kristy went on, clearing her voice. "We want to make sure you can ride Skipper—he bolted the last time."

"Of course I can—" Alison started.

"Then come out to our ranch on Wednesday," Kristy interrupted. "It's on Bighorn Road, just up from the Bar Q, the second-last place on the left. Two o'clock, okay?"

"I'll be there! Thanks."

"Yeah." Kristy's voice was flat. "Bye."

Alison put down the phone, tingling all over. Imagine that kid's nerve, thinking she couldn't ride Skipper. She wanted that horse and she was going to get him. There was just one small matter.

Twenty thousand dollars. In two days!

That night, Alison cleared the dishes off the dinner table. "That was a delicious dinner, Mom," she said. "You know, I really like having the time to eat with you like this."

Marion looked up in surprise. "Thank you, Alison."

Alison sat down with her elbows on the table and her chin in her hands. "Can we just sit and talk for a while?"

"Of course."

"I feel like I don't get enough time to talk to you, you know, about your job and stuff. How's it going?"

"My job?" Marion smiled. "You're not really interested in my job."

"Sure I am!" Alison smiled back. "I know I've been a

bit focused on myself lately, but I really want to know about you."

"Well—" Marion nodded, "actually, it's going really well. They're talking about sending me overseas on a sales trip soon. Maybe Japan."

"Wow! That would be fabulous." Alison got up. "Would you like some coffee, Mom?"

"Sure, that would be great. And how are things going with you?"

"Fine." Alison walked slowly to the coffee maker. "I've found the horse I'd like. Now all I need is twenty thousand dollars."

She could hear her mother's gasp over the sound of water running into the pot. "Twenty thousand? You know what I've said about buying a horse. Any horse. But a twenty thousand dollar horse is utterly out of the question."

"But I could get a horse, if I could afford it?"

"I suppose so ..." Her mother shook her head. "But this is a fantasy!"

"Maybe not." Alison turned on the coffee maker.

"What do you mean?"

"I talked to Dad." Alison came back to the table. "He's willing to give me half."

"Ten thousand dollars!" Her mother's voice rose dangerously. "He doesn't want to send me support payments, but he'll give you ten thousand dollars?"

Alison sighed, looking down. "I guess he still feels guilty about selling Duchess without telling me."

There was a silence.

"But you shouldn't feel guilty about my losing Duchess, Mom." Alison reached for her hand. "I know you wouldn't have done such a mean thing on your own."

Marion cleared her throat. "That's just half the money you'd need."

"I know." Alison looked up with a wistful grin. "But I have two thousand in my savings account. And Grandmother Chant will send me sixteen hundred for my birthday in October—one hundred for every year of my life."

"You still need over six ..." Marion was calculating.

"I know. But if I get a part-time job once school starts, I could pay you back." Alison begged with her eyes. "Mom, if I had this horse, Skipper, I'd be so happy. I'd promise to work for an entrance scholarship to college—that would mean my first year would be almost free—and I'd keep my room clean and help with housework. We'd show Dad we were really independent!"

There was another silence. "This is important to you, isn't it?" her mother asked.

"More than anything in the world!"

"And you think you can find a place to keep it—this horse? And work to pay for its board?"

"I'm sure I can! I'll teach riding again, like I did at home."

A guilty pang crossed her mother's face when Alison tossed off the word "home."

"I'd have to take out a loan." Marion shook her head. "Six thousand dollars."

# CHAPTER 10

# IS THIS THE GIRL?

"What's Craig doing today?" Alison asked Chuck. She tried to make it sound casual.

It was Wednesday and they were on their way to the Double J. When Alison told Chuck about the arrangement to buy Skipper, he had taken time off from his work at the Bar Q to drive her to the Joneses' for her test ride.

"Do you mean why isn't Craig coming with us?" Chuck teased. "I guess he was too busy to come on a fool's errand. The real question is why I agreed to drive you out here myself."

"Why wouldn't you?" Alison grinned at him. "You're my friend."

"Because you can't buy Skipper Bug." Chuck glanced at her. "Even if you can ride him, where are you going to get twenty thousand dollars?"

"I've already got it," Alison said smugly.

"How?" Chuck's eyes were two round circles of surprise.

"Watch the road!" Alison shouted. Chuck spun the wheel, and the truck lurched back to the center.

"I asked my dad." Alison hunched down in the truck seat. "He wasn't very friendly, at first, but he came around. He'll give me half."

"Ten thousand?" Chuck shook his head. "Your parents spoil you."

"No—" Alison shrugged, "they owe me."

"You still need another ten thousand," Chuck reminded her.

"I get money from my grandmother for my birthday and I've got some savings," Alison explained. "Plus, I bribed my mom for the rest."

"What do you mean, 'bribed'?" Chuck hit the brakes as they corkscrewed around a bend in the narrow road.

"Simple." Alison shrugged again. "I told her I'd get a job and top marks in school, so I can get a good scholarship to college—that'll save lots of money. I also promised to be positive and cheerful about living in Horner Creek. And keep my room clean," she added.

Chuck shoved his hat up his forehead. "Remind me to come to you when I need financial advice. But you don't actually have much of this money yet—it's all promises."

"I'm good for it," Alison said in an outraged voice. "Kristy Jones will get her money, eventually."

"I have a feeling she might want it sooner than eventually," Chuck muttered as they came to a leaning mailbox by the side of a dirt lane. "This place looks like it could use some quick cash." He pulled the truck over.

"What are you doing? Why are you stopping?" cried Alison. "It says Double J on the mailbox."

"I'm stopping because I'm going to try one last time to change your mind." Chuck's eyes narrowed. "Look at this place." He pointed to the dilapidated buildings in the distance. "Did you ever think that Kristy might not want to sell her horse? That her dad might have forced her to say yes because they need the money?"

"So?" Alison knit her eyebrows into a frown.

"So, do you really want Skipper Bug if it's going to make someone else unhappy? How would you feel if you were Kristy?"

"If Skipper was my horse, I'd figure out a way to keep him," Alison said firmly. "I wouldn't let anyone take him away. Come on. Let's go."

"All right." Chuck put the truck in gear and turned down the Double J driveway. "But you know how we talk about our bossy grandparents?"

"Sure." Alison looked at him sharply. "Why are we talking about them now?"

"Because sometimes," Chuck said, "I think you might turn into one of those bossy people yourself."

"Chuck!" Alison exploded, "stop lecturing me like a big brother."

"All right, but you're making a mistake." He jammed his hat back down to his bushy red eyebrows and glared at the lane ahead.

Kristy saw the blue pickup with its cloud of dust coming down the lane.

"They're here, Pop," she called.

Her father came out of the barn, walking slowly. "They didn't bring a trailer."

"We're gonna see if she can ride Skipper first, remember?" Kristy insisted. "I'm not letting him go if she can't."

Her father gave a quick nod. "All right. You get her all set up. I'll come and watch her ride." He turned and shuffled toward the house.

Kristy knew he was embarrassed about having to sell Skipper. But Pop is already counting on the money, Kristy thought. He'd looked better ever since he got the news Skipper could be sold. Her heart felt torn in two—she loved them both so much.

"Come on, Skipper, you're on display," she murmured to her horse. She'd groomed Skipper's chestnut hide till he gleamed. His hooves were polished, his mane combed. He looked like the champion he was, Kristy thought proudly.

At the same time, a little voice inside her was whispering, I hope you throw that snob in the dirt! As she watched Alison slide from the front seat and brush the dust from her hat, all her dislike welled up. Why should this girl have everything? Why could she snap her fingers and offer so much money for Skipper? For her, barrel racing was just a game.

Skye came running from the house and put her hand in Kristy's. "Is this the girl who's going to take Skipper?" she said, just loud enough for Kristy to hear.

"If she can ride him." Kristy squeezed Skye's hand.

"I hope she's a horrible rider," hissed Skye fiercely.

"So do I, but promise me you won't do anything to spook Skipper." Kristy looked into her sister's small, determined face. "This is important. Promise!"

"All right." Skye's face fell. She took a handful of burrs out of her pocket. "I was going to put these under his saddle blanket."

"Well, don't." Kristy grabbed the burrs. "We have to play fair."

To Alison she said, "We set up some barrels in the paddock. Want to tack Skipper up and ride him around them?"

## CHAPTER 11

# AROUND THE BARRELS

Alison took Skipper's lead rope and led him into the barn.

So far, so good. He walked into the crossties like a school horse who'd been saddled and bridled by strangers all his life.

What a dump this barn is! Alison thought. The stalls had all been cribbed, the roof was sagging and all the equipment was old, old, old. Skipper's saddle and bridle were old and worn, too, but spotless. Alison smoothed the blanket on his back, hoisted the saddle up high and let it down gently in the center of his back.

She kept an eye on Skipper's ears. They were back a little, in protest, but not lying flat against his head as they would if he was really annoyed.

"It's okay, big fella," Alison soothed as she reached under his belly for the cinch. "I won't tighten your cinch till we're all ready to ride. So don't blow up your belly on me."

She knew he was watching her, getting a fix on this new person. She was determined to start off on the right foot, so she kept her body bent away from him, kept out of his face, didn't look directly at him. I'm a non-threatening human being, she wanted to tell him with her body language, but I know what I'm doing and I won't take any bad manners from you.

Alison undid the crossties and slipped his bridle on with a practiced hand. "Let's go, my beauty," she murmured, and Skipper Bug walked peacefully beside her.

For today, Alison had worn jeans and boots with a good heel. She wasn't taking any chances on slipping out of the saddle or getting her foot stuck in the stirrup this time. As she led Skipper through the paddock gate, Alison saw that the ground was rough and the barrels spaced closer together than in competition.

"We'll take it nice and slow," Alison promised Skipper. "No fancy stuff." At the same time, she was determined to let Kristy and her father know that she could ride Skipper around the barrels in perfect safety.

Out of the corner of her eye, she saw her audience— Chuck, taller than the rest, beside an older man who must be Kristy's dad, then Kristy and her sister, Skye. They leaned on the fence, silent but focused.

They all expect me to fail, Alison thought suddenly. I'll show them!

Alison knew she could ride. She'd been winning dressage competitions since she was seven. She just had to convince Skipper that she respected him but that she was the boss.

After swinging herself into the saddle, Alison took control by bending Skipper into a turn right away. She kept her hands soft and her body balanced. Paying close attention to his ears and tail, she walked him until his body relaxed.

All right, now, she told him with her legs and hands, a nice easy lope to the first barrel. Alison knew that any small mistake and she could be in the dirt. Fine, she wouldn't make a mistake. She guided Skipper around the first barrel, letting him have lots of room.

"That's right, now the second barrel—same way." Skipper collected himself for the turn, forgetting the new rider on his back. Who said this was a problem horse? Alison rejoiced. He's a dream to ride! They loped to the third barrel, made a nice turn and headed back toward the watchers by the fence.

Alison could feel Skipper stretch out to run, so she squeezed the reins to let him know there would be no dash for the finish. As they reached the fence, she sat deep in her seat and said, "Whoa. Good boy. That was perfect!" She leaned forward to pat his neck.

Alison glanced at Kristy and quickly looked away— there was such a mixture of pride and heartbreak on her face. Skye was looking down at her boots, and Chuck was shaking his head. The only person who seemed even slightly happy was Kristy's dad, who was beaming at Skipper.

"That was a good ride," he said, tipping back his battered cowboy hat. "I'm Mike Jones, Kristy's father."

Alison slid off Skipper and led him to the fence. She stuck out her hand to Mr. Jones. "Thank you. I'm Alison Chant."

"I understand you want to buy this horse." He shook her hand with his rough one, then turned to his daughter. "Kristy, are you satisfied she can handle him?"

Kristy's thin face was white. "Yeah, she can ride him fine." The words seemed wrenched out of her.

"When would you be wantin' the deal to go through?" Mike asked.

Alison gulped. "Right away. I'd like to enter him in the big Labor Day race in Digby, a week and a half from now."

Mike looked at the ground. "Right away, you say?"

Alison patted Skipper's neck. "Yes. I'd like to get him used to me before the race."

"Of course, there's the money, and transfer of papers ..." Mike began.

"If you have the papers ready by Saturday, I'll make sure my mom gets a certified check for the twenty thousand," Alison said firmly.

She could see Chuck rolling his eyes.

"Where are you going to keep this wonder horse once you get him?" Chuck asked on the way back to town.

"I've thought about that," Alison told him. "I'll ask Sara Kelly if we can keep him at their ranch. That's where we boarded Shadow last winter and spring. They've got a good arena for practicing."

"How will you get there?" Chuck stared at the road ahead.

"It's not that far—I can take the bus."

"Got it all planned," he muttered.

"I have," sighed Alison. "There's just one small detail—how to get Mom to get that certified check by this weekend. I really want to pick up Skipper Bug on Saturday."

Chuck threw back his head and laughed. "Only you would call a check that big a small detail."

"Chuck," Alison burst out, "you're always criticizing me! Why do you hang around me if you disapprove of everything I do?"

He glanced at her, sitting so proud and straight. "I don't know why." He shook his head. "Maybe I'm just curious to see how it all comes out."

"Why didn't he buck her off?" Tears streamed down Skye's cheeks. "You should have let me put burrs under his saddle!"

"He was only good because there were no other horses around." Kristy's face was pressed to Skipper's shiny neck.

"That was your one chance," she whispered. "Now you have to go."

How could poor Skipper understand that he'd be taken away to live in another stable, ridden by another rider and never see her again? He had no idea what he'd done by behaving so nicely for Alison!

"C'mon," her father said tiredly, "it's been a big afternoon—let's go see about some dinner."

Kristy took a long, deep sniff of Skipper's good horse smell and turned away. She must not show her feelings to her father. "Sure, Pop, I'll be right there. I'll come back and feed you later," she promised Skipper. "I'll spend as much time as I can with you before Saturday." Kristy knew, no matter what she did, that day would come too soon.

"Don't cry in front of Pop," she said sharply to Skye as they followed their father to the house. "There'll be other horses."

"Not like Skipper," wailed Skye.

## CHAPTER 12

# PICKING UP SKIPPER

Alison called the Bar Q that night, looking for Chuck.

The phone rang five times before it was picked up. "Hel-lo."

"Chuck!" Alison exclaimed. "I've got a huge problem! Sara Kelly is off barrel racing and her brother Rob is still up at Mustang Mountain. I'm not going to be able to keep Skipper there—they aren't boarding horses right now."

"It's ... uh ... not Chuck," came an apologetic voice. "This is Craig."

There was stunned silence. "Oh, I'm sorry."

"That's all right."

Now that she really listened, Craig's voice was younger and higher than Chuck's. "Is Chuck there?" Alison asked. "I have to talk to him."

"No, he's gone to Calgary with Grandfather," said Craig. "Look, why don't you keep your horse here at the Bar Q? Granddad's got lots of room in the barn, and I'm sure he'd be glad to have him."

Alison gasped. "Are you sure? I mean, that would be ... great, but the Bar Q is a long way from here, and I don't drive."

"No problem." Craig laughed. "I can drive you out whenever you want."

Alison's head reeled with the possibilities. Her horse stabled at the Bar Q. Rides to the ranch with Craig. "I— thank you, Craig," she stammered. "But I'll still have to talk to Chuck and your grandfather."

Why hadn't Chuck offered to keep Skipper at the Bar Q in the first place? she wondered. Maybe because he disapproved of the whole deal.

"I'm sure my grandfather would be happy ..." Craig repeated.

Of course he would—Alison remembered that Grandfather McClintock was determined to push them together. She was just as determined not to let him. "I'll think about it," she gulped. "I have to find a stable before Saturday."

By Friday, she'd decided. She had no other place to keep Skipper. The Bar Q would have to do until she found another stable that was closer—meanwhile, she would keep Craig at a distance. She just wished she could keep the echo of his voice out of her mind.

On Saturday, Chuck agreed to meet Alison and her mother at the Double J with his horse trailer so he could move Skipper to the Bar Q. They would drive out with the certified check.

"I can't believe you've talked us into spending twenty thousand dollars on a barrel racing horse!" Marion stormed on the way to the bank. "And why on earth does everything have to be in such a rush? The only branch open on Saturday is in the opposite direction from the ranch. By the time we get the check certified, we're going to be late."

We can't be late! Alison thought. Chuck would be waiting. Kristy and her dad would be waiting, with Skipper. She wanted the sale to go smooth as silk—no hitches.

"It isn't my fault you had to work so much this week and couldn't go to the bank," she muttered. "And Grandmother Chant didn't send my birthday money until yesterday."

"And why should she? Almost two months early?" Marion's voice was rising.

"I want to race Skipper in Digby, on September fourth," Alison struggled to explain. "I need him now if I'm going to have time to practice."

"But getting all this money together in two days!" her mother cut her off. "Getting a loan approved—"

"I'll pay you back, I swear, Mom," Alison promised. "I'll get a job, and anyway, Skipper will win lots of money barrel racing. He won a thousand dollars the first time I saw him race."

"You're counting your chickens before they hatch." Her mom sighed.

Once they reached the bank, everything took place in slow motion. There was a long lineup for the teller, then processing the check took half an hour. Alison shifted from one foot to the other, silently begging the clock to slow down and the bank people to hurry, hurry!

Finally, Alison's mom handed her a white envelope. "Okay, here's the check. That horse better be worth it."

"Wait till you see him." Alison breathed a sigh of relief, hugging the precious envelope.

"I can't stay—I have a meeting. Can Chuck bring you home after you get the horse settled at his place?"

"Probably." Alison gave her mother a disappointed glance. "Mom, the horse's name is Skipper Bug." Her mom could have planned to take a few minutes to meet him, she thought.

But as they drove toward the Double J, Alison could feel waves of anger and resentment coming off her mother like steam from a simmering pot. "If only ..." Marion started to say, then shook her head and bit her lip.

"What?" Alison stared at her mother's stern profile. "If only what?"

"Never mind." Her mom shook her head again and burst out, "If only you'd stuck with dressage!"

"You mean, if only I'd won big dressage competitions, Dad wouldn't have sold Duchess ... and I wouldn't have adopted Shadow from the mustang program in Wyoming ... and you and Dad would never have had that terrible fight with Grandmother Chant, and you'd still be together and we'd be living in New York? Is that it?" The words gushed from Alison like water from a burst pipe. Was that what her mother thought? That everything that had happened in her life since last fall was her fault?

"Don't be so dramatic." Her mother turned to her. "Just be really sure this Skipper Bug is the horse you want and he's going to make you happy, that's all."

"He will." Tears bit at the back of Alison's eyes. She looked out the window over the green hills and mountains in the distance. "I know he will."

She was still feeling the sting of this conversation when her mother dropped her at the Double J Ranch and sped back down the laneway. It made her annoyed at Chuck's freckles and blind to Kristy's sorrowful face.

Chuck soothed Kristy as Skipper Bug was loaded into the trailer. "We're just down the road—you can visit Skipper anytime. I'll bet he'd like that."

"He's my horse," Alison muttered to him. "Don't encourage her to think he isn't."

Chuck went on talking to Kristy as if she hadn't spoken. "Don't worry, we'll take good care of him at the Bar Q. Skipper will be pampered like a prince."

Kristy nodded but didn't say a word.

Skye jumped into the trailer to give Skipper one last kiss on his nose. "I don't want you to go," she wailed.

"Come on, kiddo." Mike Jones climbed in after Skye, lifted his daughter in his arms and carried her out of the trailer. "It's time to say good-bye."

Alison thrust the white envelope at Kristy. "Here's your money."

Kristy jerked back, as if the envelope burned her fingers. "Give it to my dad. It's for him, and the ranch."

Alison swallowed hard. "All right." She turned to Kristy's father, still holding Skye. "Here, Mr. Jones. It's a certified check for twenty thousand dollars."

He took the check but didn't smile. "Take good care of Skipper," he said. "He's a fine horse."

Later that afternoon, Skipper paced a large box stall in the Bar Q barn. The tall chestnut shook his head, nervous in his new surroundings, whinnying for Kristy or a familiar face.

"I think I'll wait until tomorrow to ride him," Alison told Chuck. "He'll be settled by then."

"Sure, he's going to be happy as a clam here."

Chuck was still mad at her, Alison realized. His voice had a nasty, sarcastic edge. She'd hoped to get things straight with him now they were at the Bar Q. But Chuck's green eyes were still scrunched up, and he hadn't smiled at her once as he forked bedding into Skipper's stall.

"Kristy says Skipper's not good with other horses, so we'll keep him by himself for a while, right?" She tried to coax him into conversation.

Chuck nodded. "I think he and Lucky Ralph might get along, but we'll take it slow."

Alison had forgotten all about the skinny bay Chuck had rescued. "How is Lucky Ralph?"

Chuck thrust the pitchfork hard into the wheelbarrow. "Stop trying to soften me up!" He glared at her. "How could you act so—so cold to Kristy—back there at her ranch?"

Alison felt her face flush. "She wanted to sell the horse. I wanted to buy him. She didn't even seem grateful for the money, after all the trouble I went to to get that check!"

"She didn't want to sell him." Chuck's voice was hoarse with anger. "She had to sell him because her father has a bad heart."

"Oh ..." Alison faltered. "I didn't know."

"That's no excuse for acting like an ice princess." Chuck shook his head and went back to forking hay. "Sometimes I'm ashamed of you."

"If you think I'm so evil, why don't you leave me alone?" Alison spun away from him, hurt by his words. She was sorry about the Jones family, but Chuck didn't need to talk to her like that! She stared into Skipper Bug's stall. There was no sound in the big barn except for the scraping of Chuck's pitchfork, and Skipper's pacing.

Then Alison heard soft footsteps behind her.

"Hi."

Alison whipped around to see Craig. He was walking toward her the way she'd first seen him, with the light behind him and a smile that made her knees go weak.

Chuck stopped in mid-swing. "What are you doing here?" he growled.

"Don't wave that fork at me. It's sharp!" Craig laughed. "Grandfather thought Alison might like a lift back to town since I'm going right past Horner Creek on my way home."

"Uh, I don't know." Alison glanced at Chuck. "Maybe I should stay here, with Skipper."

"How is your new horse?" Craig came to stand beside her and peer into Skipper's stall. "Why is he pacing and bobbing his head? He looks totally miserable in there."

Chuck mumbled, "He's missing Kristy and her family. It won't make any difference if Alison hangs around."

Alison had suddenly had enough of Chuck and his snide remarks. "A lift home would be great," she announced. "Thanks, Craig."

She stalked out of the barn, with Craig behind her.

His Japanese sports car, pale yellow, was parked near the house. As she stepped into it, Alison saw Grandfather McClintock on the front porch, grinning like a bandit who'd just robbed a bank.

"Look at that old man," she whispered. "He planned this!"

"Did you say something?" Craig slipped into the driver's seat.

"It's a nice car!" Alison blurted. "Is it yours?"

"No, it's my mom's." Craig grinned. "She lets me use it when she doesn't need it. I just got my license a month ago."

His grin had the usual effect on her insides. As they headed down the long Bar Q driveway, Alison vowed to concentrate on Skipper all the way to Horner Creek. Concentrate on not falling madly in love with Craig McClintock.

"Can we get something straight?" Craig asked after a few minutes of driving. "Are you Chuck's girl, or not?"

"Not." Alison spat out the word. "Chuck and I are friends, that's all." Sometimes we're not even friends, she added to herself.

"That's good." Craig turned to her. "So he won't get jealous if I keep driving you out to the ranch and home again?"

"Why should he?" Alison asked crossly.

"Awesome!" Craig leaned toward her. "Does that mean you'll go out with me? How about tonight? It's Saturday."

## CHAPTER 13

# TRAINING SESSIONS

"I can't go out with anybody, right now." Alison could feel herself blush. "I have to get Skipper ready for our first race." The idea of going out with Craig gave her goosebumps, but she knew she'd never be able to focus on Skipper's training if she agreed. Besides, she hated to give his grandfather the satisfaction of being right! She could still see the old man's face, gloating as they drove away together.

"Sure." Craig sighed. "I understand. There's no rush. It must be tough, breaking in a new horse. Maybe another time."

The rest of the way to town, they talked about autumn coming, school starting in a couple of weeks, anything to avoid the fact that Craig had just asked her out, and she had put him off.

Alison would be in grade eleven at Horner Creek High School, Craig in his final year at a private school in Calgary.

"I want to go to college back east," Alison told him. "That's where I really belong."

"I'll be going to school in the east, too," said Craig. "Chuck seems to hate the idea of going to McGill, but I think it'll be exciting, living in Montreal, so close to New York."

"You and Chuck are nothing alike." Alison grinned. They were pulling up in front of her townhouse. "Thanks for the lift."

"Anytime." Craig's smile turned up the corners of his mouth adorably. "Let me know when you want to go out to the ranch again."

Alison waved as she watched Craig zip away in his mother's sports car. Keeping her distance from him was going to be harder than she thought. Especially if he was driving her to the Bar Q to see Skipper. She was still shivering from the thrill of him asking her out.

Her mother turned from the window as she walked in. "That was a different boy."

"Yup." Alison headed for her room.

"Wait a minute," her mother called. "I want to know who you're going out with!"

"I'm not going out with anyone, Mother." Alison tried to stay polite. "Craig just gave me a ride home from the

Bar Q since you had a big important meeting and couldn't be bothered to wait."

"Who's Craig?" Her mother's eyes drilled holes.

"Craig McClintock." Alison sighed. "Chuck's cousin. His younger cousin," she added, knowing her mother would ask.

"Well, all right." Marion dropped the attack. "As long as it's one of the McClintocks. They seem like a good family."

"You mean you've heard they have bags of money, don't you?" Alison couldn't resist. "You wouldn't care if they held up corner stores as long as they were rich."

"Alison—that's not fair!"

"You're right," Alison apologized. "It's just that it's complicated dealing with the McClintocks. I wish I didn't have Skipper stabled at their ranch."

Early the next morning, Alison begged her mom to drive her out to the Bar Q so she wouldn't have to call Craig. He made her feel dizzy and confused, and she needed to be calm to face Skipper.

"All right, but it will have to be right away," her mother grumbled. "I have a business brunch."

It was a bright August Sunday, and the face of the Rockies was rosy in the morning sun as they drove west toward Kananaskis Country.

"Thanks," Alison said as she hopped out of the car. "You don't have to come and get me—I'll ask Chuck for a ride home." If he's speaking to me, she added to herself.

She found Chuck in the barn, mucking out Skipper's stall. He looked surprised to see her. "I didn't know you got up this early," he commented.

"Look, Chuck, I don't need any more of your smart remarks," Alison blazed. "Where's Skipper?"

Chuck shrugged. "Come and see your big fella."

Alison followed him to a large paddock behind the main barn. Skipper was head down in a pile of hay, munching contentedly. On the other side of the pile was Lucky Ralph.

"These two are getting along really well," Chuck said. "Lucky doesn't seem to agitate Skipper the way other horses do."

"That's Lucky." Alison smiled at her own joke. Was she imagining it, or had Chuck thawed a little since yesterday?

He turned to her. "I still don't like the idea of you riding him in the barrel race next weekend. Don't you think it's too soon?"

"No, I don't." Alison shook her dark head firmly. "And I'd like to work with him alone for a while. Have you got a round pen?"

"S-sure ..." Chuck hesitated. "It's right over there. Want me to catch him and put him in there for you?"

"No," Alison said again. "Just show me where to get a halter and a lunge line, and I'll go get him."

Ten minutes later, Alison walked into the paddock with the halter over her shoulder. She didn't advance toward Skipper, just stood back and watched him. How beautiful he was—a lovely light chestnut with a matching mane and tail. He had the powerful hindquarters of a good barrel horse and strong, straight legs.

He lifted his head from the hay, watching Alison. "I know you're missing Kristy," she began to talk to him in a low voice. "You're a horse without a leader, and you need that. I can be your leader. You can trust me." She turned and walked away from him, hoping he'd follow out of curiosity.

Sure enough, as she reached the fence, Skipper was right behind her. "So you came to check me out," she continued talking. "That's good. Now let's slip on this halter, get in the round pen and do some work."

Alison knew if she had control of Skipper on the ground, things would be easier when she was on his back. He needed to stop when she wanted him to stop, not when he decided it was a good idea. He had to learn not to bolt when he was startled or afraid. She'd seen him in the alley, twice, at the beginning of races, charging and plunging and almost out of control. Kristy could barely contain him. That wasn't good.

"This is school," she told Skipper as she attached the lunge line to his halter in the pen. "I'm the teacher, so pay attention." She led Skipper to the fence, where Chuck handed her a long whip with a white plastic flag on the end. Skipper swung away at the sight of the whip.

"It's okay," Alison soothed. "I'm not going to hit you with this. Just give directions."

She worked with him for half an hour, until he was following instructions well. Then she stopped before he lost his concentration and started to fool around. She ended the session with a treat and words of praise for being such a good boy.

"There, did you see that, Chuck?" Alison unclipped the lunge line from Skipper's halter and strode to the fence where Chuck was watching, her face flushed with success. "Skipper will be fine. I've got five more days to work with him." She grinned happily. "He'll be ready for Digby by Saturday."

Chuck nodded. "You know what you're doing with horses, I'll say that for you."

"Thanks," Alison said briefly. "It's all about letting them know who's boss."

She glanced over her shoulder at Skipper. He'd followed her to the fence. His head was relaxed, he was yawning and licking his lips—all signs he'd submitted to her. I am good with horses, Alison thought proudly.

"If your heart's set on taking him to that race in Digby, I'll trailer him over," Chuck offered as they walked back to the paddock with Skipper. "Craig can drive you out from town."

Craig again! Alison led Skipper through the gate Chuck held open for her. If only people and feelings were as easy to control as horses!

The training sessions with Skipper went on all week, and each day Alison felt more confident. She could not only manage the big chestnut, she could win with him!

On Saturday morning, race day, she was so excited that she forgot Craig was picking her up, forgot to fuss with her hair and put on eye makeup. For luck, she wore the same jeans and shirt she'd been wearing to train Skipper all week.

"Whew," Craig said when she hopped into the car, "now that's a nice horsy smell."

"Oh, sorry," Alison laughed. "I didn't want to change. Horses get comfortable with a person's scent, and I want Skipper to be very comfortable."

"I'll be sure to explain that to my mother when she asks who stunk up her car." Craig grinned at her.

"I gather your family isn't into horses?" Alison asked as they left Horner Creek behind and headed north.

"No, I'd say they're more urban than cowboy."

"But you still wear that big silver buckle." She pointed to Craig's elaborate belt buckle.

He smiled. "Granddad gave this to me. I wear it to the ranch, and if I'm going to a show, like today."

"So you like to please your grandfather?" Alison knew she was being nosy.

Craig didn't seem to mind. "No, he's an old man, and it doesn't hurt to make him happy."

"Chuck doesn't feel that way," Alison said. "He thinks his granddad tries to rule his life."

"Maybe because Chuck's the favorite grandson." A hint of bitterness crept into Craig's voice. "Chuck's the one who's going to take over the Bar Q. He's the rancher, the chip off the old block."

Craig turned off the highway onto a narrow paved road that ran through rolling farmland. The fields were golden this time of year and the huge sky was a dazzling blue. They drove north for almost an hour, up and down one long hill after another, chatting about unimportant things.

I feel so relaxed with him, Alison thought. She risked another question. "Do you mind that Chuck's your grandfather's favorite? Would you like to inherit the ranch?"

"That's a joke!" Craig snorted. "Can you see me running three thousand head of cattle?"

"Honestly, no. Do you want to?"

Craig shook his head. "It's just that Chuck and I have always been rivals, ever since we were little kids. He was always the big cousin who could do anything, the apple of Granddad's eye. For years, I tried to compete, tried to keep up. Now, I try to go in my own direction—anything not connected to ranching."

"I know what you mean." Alison thought of her Grandmother Chant, always trying to turn her into a proper little socialite, elegant, aloof and proud.

She glanced at Craig's profile and noticed he scrunched up his eyes the same way Chuck did when he was angry or upset. "What would you like to do?" she asked quietly.

"Promise not to tell?"

"Sure."

"McGill has a good theater program. I'd like to study ... acting." He said it as if he was confessing a secret desire to be a car thief.

"Terrific! I think you'd be great." Craig has the looks to be a movie star, Alison thought. She asked, "But why not tell? Why not tell everyone?"

"Are you kidding?" Craig pounded the steering wheel. "Granddad would throw me into a water trough if he knew I wanted to be an actor!"

"What about your parents? Don't they have something to say about all this?"

"They all pretty much dance to Grandfather McClintock's tune." Craig shrugged. "They don't think they do, but they do. We all do." He fingered his shiny belt buckle. "I guess that's the real reason I wear this."

Alison suddenly thought of something and sat up straight. "Am I another way to please your grandfather?" She put her hand on his arm. "Is that why you asked me out?"

Craig blushed. "Well, I ... uh—"

"Never mind," she interrupted him. They had just passed the sign to the Digby fairgrounds. "Turn here, we'll talk about this later." It was just as she thought. Old Mr. McClintock was behind all this. He was determined to throw her and Craig together so Chuck would go to McGill. He didn't need to worry. Chuck was disgusted with her. These days, he acted as if she made him break out in a rash. If it was ever true that she was the reason he didn't want to go east, it wasn't true anymore!

In the distance was a low barn and a collection of trucks with horse trailers. "Look," Alison shouted as they rolled into the grounds, "there's Chuck with the horse trailer, and Skipper."

She was tingling with excitement to see her big horse. How was he feeling after his trip? Would he race for her?

# CHAPTER 14

# UNLUCKY

"He's pretty agitated." Chuck stroked Skipper's neck. "It looks as though he didn't settle down the whole trip."

Alison inspected her horse. Skipper was tied to the shiny aluminum trailer. His tail was clamped close to his body, his head held high and tight, the signs, she knew, of a nervous and unhappy horse.

"I should have ridden out with him." Alison felt a guilty pang that she'd enjoyed the trip with Craig. She nudged Chuck aside and stood close to Skipper's shoulder. "He's all sweaty!" she exclaimed, feeling the damp hide under his mane.

"Like I said, he spent the whole trip working himself into a lather. Plus, it's mighty hot." Chuck glanced at the sky, which was filling with towers of white cloud. "Most likely we'll get a thunderstorm this afternoon. Horses get spooked by this kind of weather."

"He'll be fine," Alison insisted. She yanked the water bucket and a hay net from the storage locker at the back of the trailer. "Don't worry, big guy. I'll get you cooled out and comfortable before the race."

"The junior division is first." Chuck shoved his hat back. "Want to take a look at the arena? You'll be riding inside."

"No, I want to get Skipper ready," said Alison. "Can you check it out for me?"

"No problem. C'mon, Craig, I think the girl wants to be alone with her horse."

Chuck and Craig strolled away side by side. Alison glanced after them—Chuck tall and wide, with his swagger—Craig, shorter and leaner, with a straight back and long stride. It's Craig who makes my heart thump, Alison thought as she hurried to fill Skipper's water bucket at the tap nearby. Not just because he was better looking, either. Craig was easier to talk to. Not as prickly and critical as Chuck.

Still, she wished she had Chuck's respect. She wasn't sure why it mattered so much, but somehow, it did. She wished he would grin at her in the old way—the way he did before she bought Skipper.

As she walked back to the trailer, Alison kept an eye out for Kristy and her little sister. Would they come to watch her race Skipper, she wondered, or stay away?

Kristy Jones was far from the Digby fairgrounds at that moment.

She was slumped in a hard chair, clutching her sister's hand. They had brought their father to the hospital that morning—phoned for an ambulance before breakfast, when they couldn't wake him.

Now they had to sit there, in the cold hospital corridor, and wait.

"Wait here," the doctor had said. "I'll come and talk to you soon."

"Wait here," the nurse had repeated. "I'm calling your mother. Don't wander off," she'd added. "We need to be able to find you."

That had been long minutes ago—it felt like an hour. They were hungry, and Skye had to go to the bathroom.

"It's right over there." Kristy pointed to the sign on the door. "I'll watch while you go in."

"Come with me?" Skye tugged at her hand.

"I can't. The nurse said to stay here."

"I don't want to go alone."

Kristy thought of calling for the nurse, but she knew her voice would sound loud and strange in the bare, empty hall, and she was afraid. She was so afraid, but there was nothing she could do but sit there, hold Skye's hand and wait for someone to come. She wouldn't feel so bad if she were home, and Skipper was there. She thought about stroking his silky neck and feeling his soft lips nibble carrots from her hand and had such a moment of longing for her horse that she almost cried.

Chuck and Craig prowled the dim arena, where men were setting up the electronic eye on a tripod. A noisy green tractor was circling, dragging a rake to smooth the sand. Most of the light in the building came from the large open doorway at one end. Temporary pens for the horses had been set up just inside, forming an alley for the horses to start the race.

Chuck pointed to the pens. "I don't like it. It's dangerous to have Skipper start with all the other horses milling around on either side of him."

"Barrel racing is dangerous?" Craig raised an eyebrow.

Chuck snorted. "Is driving that car of yours 90 miles an hour around sharp curves dangerous?"

"Come on, it can't be that bad or people wouldn't let little kids do it," laughed Craig. "I see ten-year-olds out there getting ready to barrel race."

"People let their kids ride bucking broncs and bulls, too," Chuck reminded him. "And some of those ten-year-olds can beat the adults in barrel racing. I wouldn't worry so much, except Alison doesn't know this horse."

"She seems pretty confident ..." Craig grinned.

"That's even worse," sighed Chuck. "She shouldn't be. I've seen Skipper out of control, and he's a powerful brute."

They walked back to the trailer through a crowd of horses and riders warming up for the junior race.

Alison had Skipper saddled and was ready to go. "Good, you're back," she barked. "What does the arena look like?"

"Fairly tight, good footing, but the problem is the horses will all be bunched around the alley when you start." Chuck described the scene. "I hope you and Skipper are in the first group, so he won't have to wait too long."

Alison nodded. She put her left foot in the stirrup and swung into the saddle. "I'll warm him up here, where it's not so crowded." She leaned down to say to Chuck, "When you hear we're up next, give me a signal."

"Sure." Chuck watched her circle Skipper away from the trailers to a quiet strip of ground along the fairground fence.

"She says she's not your girl, but you seem kind of involved," Craig said, glancing at his cousin's worried face.

"Yeah," Chuck groaned. "I don't know what it is about Alison. She let me know from the minute we met that she couldn't stand the sight of me, but there's something about her ..."

"She's kind of young for you," Craig commented.

"I know that, too," Chuck agreed. "I don't so much like her as a girlfriend—it's more like Alison's a stray calf in trouble and I have to keep her from running off a cliff."

"She better not hear you comparing her to a calf," snorted Craig.

"That's just it!" Chuck exclaimed. "She puts on this tough show, but underneath she's kind of all alone and needs protecting."

Craig grinned. "You always did like taking care of orphan animals." He looked seriously at his red-headed cousin. "I hope you mean it, because I like Alison. She's one of the first girls I can really talk to. I hope she'll go out with me, once this horse-crazy phase is over."

"I wouldn't count on it being over any time soon," Chuck muttered, watching Alison exercise Skipper along the fence. Every bit of her slender body was focused on the horse, from the angle of her dark head to the tips of her boots. He shook his head. "Let's go see when she and Skipper are set to race."

At the hospital, the doctor was bending over Kristy, speaking low, so Skye, who was playing with magazines on the waiting room table, couldn't hear.

"Your father needs an operation on his heart," the doctor said. "And we need your mother to sign the consent papers."

Kristy gulped. "Can't I sign them?"

"I'm afraid you're too young, and she is his next of kin."

Kristy gulped again. She didn't like the sound of that "next of kin," like her pop was already dead!

"Don't worry," the doctor said kindly, "we've got your father stabilized, so he's not in immediate danger, and I'm sure they'll reach your mother soon. In the meantime, is there anyone you can call to come and get you? It might be a long wait for you and your sister ..." He gestured around the barren hospital.

"I'm staying right here." Kristy gave him a hard look. Then her voice faltered. "But Skye, maybe she shouldn't stay. I'll try to think of someone back home who could come and get her."

"Good." The doctor nodded. "You can use the phone at the nurses' station over there. And ask them for a sandwich and juice if you get hungry."

Hungry! The word made Kristy's stomach contract. She hadn't eaten since last night. "Thank you," she murmured, then felt a stab of guilt. How could she think of food when her father was so sick? "Will Pop be all right?"

"We're pretty sure he will." The doctor looked her in the eye, and Kristy thought he was telling the truth. "Once he gets this operation, he should make a good recovery."

"But you need to get hold of my mother so she can sign!" Kristy felt a surge of anger at her mom. Why wasn't she here when they needed her?

The nurse came bustling up. "Can you think of any other number where we could reach Mrs. Jones?" she asked Kristy. "We're not having any luck with this number."

"Bad luck. You and Skipper don't race till near the end of the pack." Chuck hurried up to tell Alison. "But they want all riders at the gate now."

"We'll be fine." Alison's voice was icy crisp. "Don't look so nervous—you're scaring my horse."

"Right. I'll stay out of your way." Chuck backed off, holding up one hand. "Have a good run."

"That's better." Alison gave him a thin smile. "See you after we win this race."

Chuck bit back the words he wanted to shout: Don't try to win. It's your first race on Skipper. Just try for a good clean run—and be careful! With Alison, that would be as much use as pouring gasoline on a fire. It would only make her more determined to ride Skipper flat out. He watched her ride toward the arena, back straight and head high. She was brave as a mountain lion, that girl.

Near the entrance, Alison got off Skipper and walked him through the jostling crowd of horses and riders and the large open doors. A chest-high steel pipe gate kept non-competitors out. Inside the gate, more steel pipes formed two oddly shaped pens, one on either side.

Skipper pulled back, not wanting to enter the pen with the other horses.

"You can do it." Alison spoke in her low, firm trainer's voice. Skipper swiveled one ear in her direction as if to say, "I hear you, but I hate this."

He pinned his ears back as she led him close to another horse and tied his lead rope to the pipe. She could feel shivers of anger and confusion sweep down his body, and she pressed close to him, hoping he wouldn't swing around and kick, or tear at another horse with his teeth. Just let it be their turn, soon!

She heard the loudspeaker announce rider after rider, heard the noise of the crowd, the pounding of hooves, the shouting of riders as they urged their horses to the finish line. Each one tightened the tension in Skipper's body till it seemed like his skin could hardly contain him. Every instinct was to bolt, run, escape.

"Soon," Alison told him finally. "We're up after this drag."

The roar of the tractor in the enclosed arena was the final insult to Skipper's ravaged senses. He stamped, whinnied and shook his head violently. "Easy!" Alison cried, afraid that he would tear the temporary fence out of the sand with each powerful toss of his head. "Look, we're going."

With fumbling fingers, she slipped off Skipper's halter and bridled him, ready to mount. When the loudspeaker announced her name, she leaped into the saddle in one flowing motion—giving him no time to think.

Then they were in flight, out of the pen, down the narrow alley, through the eye beam, streaking for the first barrel. Alison didn't have to urge Skipper on, just keep him from falling as he rounded each barrel at a steep angle. The third barrel spun and rocked but didn't fall.

They raced for the finish line. Now Alison let Skipper out into the panicked dash he'd been building. Too late, she saw a blur of green ahead. The steel gate was closed! Skipper couldn't see—the light from the open door was too bright—they were going to smash right into it.

"Whoa!" she shouted, hauling back on the rein. But Skipper was going too fast. She felt him slam into the steel pipes, felt them going over, felt herself flying free of the saddle and falling, with her horse.

Then crashing to the ground and waiting, in that heart-stopping second, for Skipper's body to slam on top of her.

She heard a thud, and shouting, then felt incredible, mind-bending pain in her forearms.

She rolled in the dirt and saw Skipper lying beside her with Chuck draped over his body. She knew without being told that the horse was badly hurt.

"Did you see that?" someone yelled. "How did he do that—keep that horse from falling right on top of her?"

"Are you all right?" She knew Chuck was calling her, but the world was spinning around, going black with pain.

# CHAPTER 15

# ALISON WAKES UP

Alison woke up in a fuzzy world of bandages and bed sheets wrapped too tight.

"Skipper?" She tried to sit. "Is Skipper dead?"

"No, he's alive," said a weary voice close to her ear.

"Oh, I'm so glad," she sighed and went back to sleep.

When she woke again, it was because her nose was itching. She tried to scratch it, only to discover that her arm was encased in heavy plaster and hurt to move. She tried her other arm, but it was the same.

"My arms," she whispered. "What's wrong with my arms?" Alison felt so dizzy and confused. The whole room was vibrating. Her mother's voice was loud and clear.

"You landed on your arms, dear," her mother said, but her mother never called her "dear." Alison tried to turn her head, but it was held tight and wouldn't move.

"Did I break my neck, too?"

"Fortunately not. They've put you in a neck brace because you wrenched something when you fell."

"Oh. It hurts. Where's Chuck?" There was something important, connected to Chuck, that she needed to remember. Alison let the memories swirl in her brain, but the last one that was clear was charging toward the green gate on Skipper's back.

"You'll see Chuck later," Marion promised.

"Where am I?" Alison asked. A wave of fear swept over her.

"Calgary Memorial Hospital—" There was a long pause. "You had surgery on your right arm an hour ago. This is the recovery room. They'll move you to your own room soon."

"Too much information ..." Alison said, and went to sleep again.

The next time she woke, they were wheeling her into a hospital elevator, and her mom was beside her. "Ouch!" Alison cried as the stretcher went over the bump at the elevator doors. She tried lifting her arms again, but they were too heavy. The casts extended higher than her elbows, so she couldn't unbend them.

"Lie still, dear," Marion murmured as the elevator doors shut. "We'll be at your room in a minute."

"Mom!" Alison panicked. "Both arms! How am I going to eat? Brush my teeth? Go to school? Go to the bathroom?"

"We'll figure it out," her mother promised. Her worried face swam into view. "Right now, we're going to get you settled in your room."

"How long do I have to stay here?" Alison gulped. She didn't like that word "settled."

Chuck was waiting in the hospital room. "Let me help," he said as they lifted her from the gurney to the bed. As soon as Alison saw his familiar face and red hair, memory came flooding back to her. Chuck, throwing himself between her and the falling Skipper.

"Chuck … I know what I was trying to remember. You saved my life."

"I just happened to be at the right place at the right time yesterday." Chuck held a drink with a flexible straw so Alison could take a sip. "They closed that gate once the race started. I guess you never noticed because you were so focused on keeping Skipper calm."

Chuck had been filling in the gaps in her memory, describing how he saw Skipper approach the gate and knew he wouldn't be able to stop. "I threw my weight against Skipper as he was falling and shoved him over," Chuck said. "If he hadn't been moving so fast, I'd never have had the strength. Something about physics ..." He smoothed back a strand of hair that had fallen over Alison's forehead.

"It was more than that." Alison desperately wanted to throw her arms around Chuck's broad body and hug him. "You were there because you were worried about us, and you saved me!" She swallowed another mouthful of water. "Just tell me, how is Skipper? He hit that gate so hard."

Chuck's cheerful face fell. "I'm not going to lie to you," he said. "Nobody knows right now how badly he's hurt. The vet is coming to check him again tomorrow. I'll give you a full report as soon as I get it."

"That doesn't sound good." Alison struggled to sit up.

Just then, a nurse came in to take her blood pressure and temperature and give her pain medication. "You shouldn't be getting Alison so agitated," the nurse said sternly. "Why don't you both have a seat in the visitors' lounge while she gets settled and has some rest."

"I'll be back later, dear," her mother whispered.

Chuck grabbed for his straw cowboy hat on the bedside table. "Me, too." He grinned as the nurse hustled them out.

Alison felt a terrible emptiness as Chuck disappeared and she was left alone in the unfriendly hospital room. She'd never realized before how gentle his big hands could be, or how he always thought about what she needed—like the way he held that drink for her. And that grin! That was the smile she'd been waiting to see again.

"What's happening to me?' Alison whispered to herself. "Is this just the painkillers?"

"I'm sorry Alison got upset," Chuck apologized as he and Marion walked down the corridor. "I didn't want to talk about Skipper, but she asked …"

"'That wretched horse!" Marion's dark eyes, so much like Alison's, were shadowed with anger. "She was so sure she wanted him, so sure she could ride him, and now she's lying here, and twenty thousand dollars is down the drain!" She saw Chuck's shocked look and stopped. "I know it's crass to worry about money right now—but it's all such a waste!"

"The—the horse isn't dead, Mrs. Chant." Chuck shifted his hat from one hand to the other. "We're hoping he'll heal."

"I don't want to discuss it!" Marion shook her head. "I hope Alison is through with this barrel racing business once and for all." She drew herself up straight with an effort. "I'm very grateful for what you did for Alison." She kept her chin high. "But I'm afraid my daughter has been out of control recently. I'd prefer it if she didn't hang around you, your cousin, your ranch or that horse from now on!"

Chuck gaped at her. "Mrs. Chant—"

Alison's mother threw out her arms. "I don't know what I'm going to do! Alison will be coming home from the hospital in a few days, and I have to go on a business trip ..." She stopped, suddenly realizing who she was talking to. "I just want to make sure she's not—you're not—I don't want her to get into any more trouble!"

"No, ma'am!" Chuck jammed his cowboy hat on his head. "She's had enough trouble already!"

"How is she?" Craig asked as Chuck squeezed himself into the small sports car outside the hospital.

"Not so good." Chuck heaved a sigh. "She came through the operation fine, but she's going to have a cast on her left arm for a couple weeks and one on her right arm for at least six weeks."

"I wish I could have seen her." Craig started the car. "I might have cheered her up."

"Sorry," Chuck mumbled, "they only allow two visitors at a time—her mom and one other. I just had to see her ..." He choked. "It's hard to look at her lying there, so helpless."

"That's tough," Craig agreed, pulling out of the parking lot. "And how's the mighty hero feeling after that daring rescue?"

"Stiff and sore." Chuck grimaced. "You know, I wasn't trying to be a hero."

"I know." Craig kept his eyes on the road. "But Alison's always going to think of you as the guy who saved her from being crushed to death under her horse. How can I compete with that?"

"How can you think about some kind of stupid competition when she's hurt like that?" Chuck growled. "Sometimes, you're as shallow as a slough. Anyway," he sighed, "neither of us has a chance with Alison. Her mother doesn't want her to see us, or the ranch, or Skipper Bug. She's got it in her head Alison's been running wild with the bad McClintock boys."

He managed a painful grin. "Poor Alison. She's got more problems than two broken arms. I always thought she exaggerated how awful her parents are, but she didn't. That mother of hers!"

## CHAPTER 16

# Surprise visitor

The next morning, the surgeon visited Alison. A slight young woman with smooth dark hair and a worried expression, she leaned over Alison, inspecting her casts.

"I'm Dr. Liu." She straightened up with a serious look. "I operated on your right arm, repairing the broken bones in your forearm—the radius and ulna."

Alison's eyebrows rose. "I broke all that?"

The doctor sat beside the bed and consulted a clipboard. "Yes. And you have damaged nerves in your arm as well. The bones, we think, will heal. The nerves, we're not so sure."

"What are you saying?" Alison wrestled herself into a sitting position so she could look the doctor straight in the face. It wasn't easy to do with two casts.

"We're not sure if you will recover the full use of your right arm. Time will tell," Dr. Liu said.

"But I'm right-handed!" Alison gasped. "I have to have the use of my arm to do everything—ride, write, everything!"

"A lot depends on your determination," the doctor said. "You need to be prepared for a long recovery and a lot of therapy."

"How long?" Alison swallowed hard.

The surgeon lifted slim shoulders. "It's difficult to be precise. Weeks, months—each case is different."

Alison wanted to scream at her, but she gulped back the angry words. She wasn't "a case," she was Alison Chant, and it was impossible that she wouldn't be able to ride again or use her right hand the way she always had.

"Do you have any feeling in your hand?"

"Yes! It hurts." Alison glared at her. To her surprise, Dr. Liu smiled.

"That's a very good sign. If your hand had no feeling, I would be more concerned."

"When do I get these casts off?" asked Alison, holding up her heavy arms, encased in plaster.

"The left one, fairly soon. The right one will take longer. The neck brace—maybe tomorrow or the next day. Try to be patient ..." She smiled again. "Are you a patient person, Alison?"

"No!" Alison burst out. "Well, I guess not." She flopped back on her pillow. "Not really."

"Then perhaps this experience will teach you a little about patience." Dr. Liu scanned her clipboard again. "It's important that you get up and walk—have you been doing that?"

"Not much," Alison confessed. "It's hard ... this stupid nightgown opens at the back, and I can't get my dressing gown on with these ..." She held up her casts again.

"We will be doing more X-rays and tests today and sending you home soon if everything looks okay," Dr. Liu said. "In the meantime, I'll send a nurse to help you get into a dressing gown, then you can go for a stroll." She looked into Alison's worried face. "I'm a skier and have had several bad injuries. I know it's frustrating, but trust your body. It's healthy and strong."

She smiled briefly once more and slipped out the door.

Alison lay back, waiting for the nurse. The doctor's words sank in slowly. Nerve damage. Losing some use of her arm. It just wasn't possible. Tears slowly oozed out of her eyes and down her cheeks into her ears. She couldn't even reach a tissue to wipe them off. She couldn't do anything without her arms.

She felt abandoned. Her mother hadn't come this morning—she'd probably gone to work. That job meant more to her than anything. And where was Chuck? He hadn't come back to visit last night, or this morning. Maybe he'd show up later, after the vet had seen Skipper ... maybe he'd bring Craig.

Alison wondered how it would be. Would her feelings for Craig be as strong when she saw the two cousins together? Maybe it was the drugs she was on, or gratitude for Chuck saving her life, but right now, it was just red-haired, smiling Charles Rodney Maxwell McClintock she longed to see.

But by four o'clock the following day, Chuck still hadn't come.

Following the doctor's orders, Alison walked down the hospital corridor from her room. She felt like an idiot, flapping down the hallway in bedroom slippers and an oversized bathrobe. Her head was still muddled with the drugs they gave her for pain. Her hair was plastered to her head, and she hadn't been able to fix it because of the casts. She took the elevator to another floor so that Chuck wouldn't see her like that—if he ever came.

On the fourth floor, Alison poked down a quiet hallway, passing hushed patient rooms and carts of bedding and equipment. All the floors were laid out in a square, so she knew that sooner or later she'd come back to the elevator. She was rounding the second corner when she almost collided with a small girl darting from a doorway with a glass in her hand.

"Kristy!" Alison gasped. "What are you doing here?"

Kristy stopped so suddenly the glass of juice in her

hand slopped over. "You!" she burst out. "My dad had an operation on his heart. I'm looking after him."

"Oh … I'm s-sorry," Alison stammered, feeling dizzy with painkillers, wishing she was anywhere but standing here looking into the furious face that stared up at her.

"What good is sorry?" Kristy gripped the glass with both hands. The words spilled out of her like acid. "You nearly killed Skipper. You took him when you couldn't even ride him, and then you raced him, and he almost died. He'll never be the same again!"

"I didn't mean—" Alison started to protest.

"Don't tell me that!" Kristy was shaking with rage. "You're greedy and selfish, Chuck says so. He says you get whatever you want 'cause you're rich. And you don't care if you wreck it."

"Chuck said that about me?" Alison stared at Kristy.

"Ask him yourself if you don't believe me," Kristy challenged. "Here he comes."

Alison turned in amazement to see Chuck hurrying toward them.

"What's going on?" He looked from Alison to Kristy and back again. The freckles stood out on his startled face. "Alison! This isn't your floor—are you all right?"

"They told me to go for a walk." Alison gulped, wanting to lean against his firm shoulder. "Wh-why are you on this floor?"

"I drove Kristy in to the hospital to visit her dad." Chuck reached out to put an arm around Alison.

"Why haven't you come to visit me?" Alison said weakly.

"Alison, there's a reason … your mother—"

"Don't try to explain." Alison cut him off, backing away. She took a deep breath to steady herself. "Kristy told me what you said about me." She turned and marched down the hall, knowing that her steps were wobbly and she looked ridiculous with her bathrobe trailing. She didn't care. All she wanted was to get back to the sanctuary of her own room, as far away from Chuck McClintock as possible!

How could he say those things about her—to Kristy?

There were people in her room when Alison reached it. Her mother met her at the door with an anxious smile. "Alison, dear, you have a surprise visitor."

Alison saw a small, bent figure at the window. It couldn't be!

The woman at the window turned around. "Sweetheart! I simply had to come."

. Alison thought she was going to faint. "Grandmother Chant," she gasped. At that moment, her grandmother was the last person on earth she wanted to see.

"I flew out here as soon as I heard about your accident." Grandmother Chant advanced on high clicking heels. "I told your mother this rough western riding was too much for you." She sniffed. "I blame her for not taking better care of my girl."

Alison's grandmother peered up into her face. She was a tiny woman, wizened from the neck down but strangely young-looking from the neck up—the result of several face-lifts. To Alison, she looked like a tiny bird of prey, ready to pounce. For as long as she could remember, her grandmother had spoken about her as if she was her personal property. It was unbelievable that she was here in this Calgary hospital.

"Sit down, Mother Chant," Marion murmured. "You must be tired."

"I'm not tired, and I won't sit down," her grandmother announced. "I think Alison should be back in New York, where they have the best doctors. She looks dreadful."

"The doctors here are excellent, Mother Chant," Marion sighed. "Besides, Alison's not well enough to travel."

"Then I'll fly in a top specialist at my expense. I want her to have the best care money can buy."

For some reason, Alison heard Kristy saying, He says you get whatever you want because you're rich. The world spun around as she struggled to her bed and lay back with her eyes shut.

"I like Dr. Liu," Alison whispered.

As usual, her grandmother paid no attention. "Your mother obviously hasn't been able to control you on her own, and now she tells me she's going on a three-week business trip to Japan." She sniffed. "I've brought enough clothes to see me into the fall and winter. If necessary, I'm staying right here until you make a full recovery."

"Mother?" Alison managed to plead. "Does she have to stay?"

"Well, really!" Grandmother Chant burst out.

"There's no one else." Marion's voice was faint. "You'll need a lot of care, and I have to travel."

A wave of nausea swept through Alison. "Help!" she muttered, trying to sit up.

"Nurse!" she heard her grandmother shout. "Get in here at once. My granddaughter is having difficulty!"

Hours later, after her mother and grandmother had gone, Alison lay staring at the pale green ceiling. It's like I'm being punished for some awful crime, she thought. What have I done that was so bad? Just fall in love with Skipper and want to race him—against Chuck's advice …

Chuck! This time, he'd completely given up on her. Alison twisted with the thought. All she could see was his startled, embarrassed face when she surprised him in the hall. He'd come to help Kristy, not her, because Kristy's dad had had a heart attack.

"He blames me for that," Alison groaned in anguish. "He's disgusted at the way I threw money at Kristy to get her to give up her horse and he warned me against racing Skipper too soon, and he was right, right, right!"

I'm a heartless, greedy person, Alison thought. I might have killed Skipper, and Chuck hates me. I deserve to be stuck with Grandmother Chant.

But I don't deserve to lose the use of my right arm! A part of Alison's weary brain rebelled.

"I will get better," she vowed to the green hospital ceiling. "And I'll barrel race again, on Skipper, if he gets better." A lump formed in her throat. Skipper had to heal—otherwise, she could never live with herself.

## CHAPTER 17

# PRISONER

Alison didn't see Chuck or Kristy for the rest of her hospital stay. Whenever she walked restlessly up and down the corridors, she stayed away from the fourth floor. She longed to know how Skipper was doing, but had no urge to face Chuck's scorn or Kristy's fury again. All she knew, thanks to her run-in with Kristy, was that Skipper had survived, but barely. It was not enough—she needed details.

Grandmother Chant came every day, chattering endlessly about everything that was wrong with the west, particularly Horner Creek. "I don't know how the two of you have managed in that shoebox of a house." She threw up her arms. "There isn't a decent closet in the place."

When Alison finally came home to the townhouse, she found it overflowing with her grandmother's belongings—seven huge suitcases. Grandmother Chant had taken over the largest bedroom, and Alison's mother was sleeping downstairs in the den.

At least her mom had some privacy.

Alison knew that her grandmother watched her every move, listened for her every sound. She found it hard to breathe because her grandmother used up all the oxygen in the house—hard to talk because she used up all the silence. Alison felt as if she was shrinking to the size of a tiny pea in the corner of her bedroom.

In the week that followed her homecoming, Alison traveled back and forth to the hospital for physiotherapy. Although it was almost the middle of September, she hadn't started school. There was no point until she had fewer treatments and the use of at least one good arm.

Once her mother left for Japan, it was up to her grandmother to drive her to therapy. One morning, Alison heard her grandmother's shrill voice on the stairs. "I see physiotherapy on the calendar for today. Are you sure? This is Saturday."

"My appointment's at one, Grandmother," Alison called back. Therapy was worth fighting for. It was working. She was out of the neck brace, and her left cast was coming off next week. Every day, she had more sensation in her right hand.

"I loathe that drive to the hospital." Her grandmother came puffing into her room. "All those freeways they call 'trails,' as if this was the set of a western movie! All those bridges. I get lost."

In New York, her grandmother didn't drive.

"I have an idea," Alison bargained as she let her grandmother help her into her jeans. "I'm sick of this suburb. After my therapy, let's drive out in the country, toward Banff. It's a nice straight road, not much traffic. You'll love it."

"I doubt it," her grandmother said shortly. "I've seen Banff. I spent a summer vacation there as a young woman." She looked critically at Alison. "But if it would please you ... I wish you'd wear skirts with elastic waists, instead of jeans. It would be much easier to get you dressed."

Alison bit her tongue, trying not to scream in frustration.

"Someone's coming, Pop." Kristy Jones stood at the kitchen window that same Saturday morning, watching a cloud of dust grow larger in the laneway. She turned to her father in the rocking chair. "Looks like a big rig of some sort."

"Better go out and see." Mike Jones smiled. It was good to see Kristy looking excited, he thought. She'd worn such a long sad face these last couple of weeks. His wife, Marta, had showed up long enough to sign the consent for his operation and look after the kids while he was in the hospital. Then she took off with little Skye.

Poor Kristy was left with nothing to do but go to school and look after a sick old man. Mike twisted irritably in his chair. He couldn't wait to get back on his feet.

Kristy ran out on the front porch. Now she could see a dark blue pickup pulling a shiny aluminum trailer through the dust. Chuck!

She ran down the front steps and met Chuck's truck as it rolled to a stop.

"Hi there," Chuck called, stepping from the truck. "I brought a friend."

Kristy stood breathless while the dust settled around the trailer's back door. She could hear a horse stamping and snorting inside. "Open it, Chuck," she pleaded. "Is it Skipper?"

"Yup, here's your buddy." Chuck undid the latch and swung open the door. "I hope you don't mind me bringing him over."

"Mind?" Kristy's face was radiant as she hopped into the back of the trailer. "I'm so glad to see him!" Her face fell as she glanced at Chuck. "Why did you bring him? Does the vet think he's hopeless?"

"No, of course not." Chuck ruffled her hair. "But Skipper's been sulky and off his food. I think he's lonely over there at the Bar Q. We can't put him with Lucky, in case they get too frisky. Skipper needs to stay quiet while his leg mends, but he also needs lots of love and attention. Think you might have time—with looking after your dad?"

"Sure, I'll have time." Kristy's face glowed with joy. She threw her arms around Skipper's neck. He turned his reddish gold head and nestled it against Kristy's stomach—he was saying hello to someone he loved and trusted.

"I'll show you what the vet said to do for him," Chuck told her as they carefully unloaded Skipper and led him into the barn. "It's just common sense, really. You have to rub liniment on his legs twice a day and hand walk him. Nothing strenuous, do you hear?"

"I promise I won't go loping him around any barrels." Kristy laughed. She led the big chestnut down the center hall to his comfortable old stall, undid the door latch and unbuckled his halter. "Look, Skipper," she said lovingly as he stuck his head in the hay net, "you're home."

"I see you kept hay in there for him." Chuck nodded. "The stall has fresh bedding, too."

"Yeah," Kristy sighed. "I guess I always hoped he'd be coming back." Her face clouded. "How long can I keep him?"

Chuck looked at Kristy's sad face and wished he could give her a better answer. "Till he heals up, I guess, or until Alison comes to get him."

Alison wished the car would steer itself right to the Bar Q, as if her wanting to see Skipper would make it magically head in that direction.

But with Grandmother Chant driving, there was no chance for magic. She drove straight and steady on the old highway to Banff, a resort town high in the Rockies. And while she drove, she talked.

"I had a very unfortunate incident at the Banff Springs Hotel when I was eighteen," she was saying. "No doubt it has prejudiced me against the Rocky Mountains, although I do love Jackson Hole, Wyoming. The spa there is wonderful." She patted her sagging neck.

Alison wasn't listening, but the mention of Wyoming made her think of Shadow, the mustang she'd adopted from a wild horse band in that state. "Do you think I could call Becky at Mustang Mountain?" she broke in. "I haven't talked to her in weeks."

"She knows about your accident," her grandmother said. "I heard Marion say she'd called her sister to tell her you'd been hurt. I understand it's awfully hard to get through to them up there."

"They have a radio-phone—" Becky started to say, but her grandmother interrupted.

"It's really such a shame Marion's sister married that dreadful cowboy. He's buried the poor woman and your cousin Becky so deep in the wilderness they can't even have a regular phone."

"Mustang Mountain is beautiful," Alison protested. "And Uncle Dan is not dreadful. Why do you hate cowboys so much, Grandmother?"

She could see her grandmother stiffen at the wheel. "The unfortunate incident I told you about at Banff Springs involved a cowboy," she murmured. "I haven't thought about it for years, but being here has brought it all back."

This was interesting. "Did you fall in love with a cowboy?"

Her grandmother sniffed, "He fell in love with me, my dear. Wanted to marry me! It was so unsuitable—a rough young man. He was ... I was ... oh, my, I don't like to think about it." She pulled the car off the road. "Time to turn around," she announced.

Alison could see that her grandmother's hands were shaking on the wheel. Never had she seen the old woman so rattled. She threw a wistful glance over her shoulder as Grandmother Chant headed back the way they'd come. The turnoff to Bighorn Road had been just ahead. They'd been so close to the Bar Q—and Skipper.

At least, she said to herself, I finally know why Grandmother hates everything western. I thought she was just an eastern snob, but there's more to it than that. I'll bet that cowboy hurt her badly. The way Chuck hurt me! her mind cried, but Alison silenced it. She didn't care about Chuck, she told herself. She wouldn't care if she never saw his ugly face again.

She tried to summon up a picture of Craig's curly dark hair and smiling eyes. He probably still liked her. But somehow, the image of Craig didn't make her tingle the way it used to.

That night, after struggling with the phone with her left hand, Alison managed to get the satellite call through to Mustang Mountain. "Oh, please answer," she begged out loud. "Please be home."

The sound of Becky's "Hello?" brought tears to her eyes.

"It's Alison!" she cried.

"Alison? This is so amazing!" Her cousin Becky's familiar voice came crackling over the line. "I just got off the phone with Chuck."

"You were talking to Chuck?" Alison swallowed hard. "What did he say? Was he—"

"Listen," Becky interrupted, "let me talk. We've got thunderstorms up here, and the line might not last and this is important ..." There was a burst of static, then Becky's voice came back on, interrupted by lightning cracks.

"Did you know that your mother ... told Chuck ... she didn't want you to see him, or Craig, or Skipper? ... That you were to keep away from the ranch?"

"No!" Alison cried. Her hand gripped the phone. "My mother! That's why I haven't heard from Chuck or Craig. Did Chuck say anything about Skipper?"

"He has bruising and pulled tendons." The phone line was breaking up. "How is life with your grandmother?" Becky shouted over the static.

"I feel like a prisoner!" Alison yelled back. "But my arms are getting better. When I see the people in physio who have spinal cord injuries, I feel lucky. At least I'm not in a wheelchair for the rest of my life."

"You sound okay." Alison could hear Becky's laugh of relief. "I've been so lonesome up here all by myself. Shadow is great. We both miss you!"

The line crackled one last time, then broke off. Alison could picture a thunderstorm sweeping down on the mountain and the cozy ranch house lit by flickering lanterns. "I miss you, too," she whispered into the phone.

She sat with the phone in her hand, remembering the last time she'd seen Chuck in the hospital. He'd been trying to explain something about her mother ... and she hadn't listened. Maybe the whole thing was a misunderstanding. She would have to see him face to face and find out.

"Did you manage to get through?" her grandmother called from downstairs.

"Just for a few minutes," Alison called back on her way to the living room. Her grandmother was sitting in front of the TV, her glasses halfway down her nose, working on a crossword puzzle. She swung her thin legs off the footstool, straightened her back and whipped off her reading glasses.

"You've come down." She peered at Alison. "Did you want something to eat?"

"No, I just thought I'd keep you company." Alison shrugged. "What's on TV?"

If she wanted to see Chuck and Skipper before her mother got home, she might need her grandmother's help. This would take patience—something, as Dr. Liu had predicted, Alison was learning from this experience.

I can start by getting Grandmother to take me to Craig's, she thought. He lives right near the hospital, and it'll be easier to face him than Chuck. I haven't seen him since before the accident, and now I know why. My interfering, bossy, miserable mother! How dare she dictate who can and who can't visit me?

CHAPTER 18

# THAT'S MY HORSE!

After a physio session the following weekend, Alison had her grandmother drop her off at Craig's. As she rang the doorbell, Alison knew she was taking a chance. Maybe he wouldn't be home. Maybe he wouldn't know how Skipper was doing, or want to talk about Chuck.

Craig answered the door with a smile that could stop traffic. "Hey! Wow! I'm glad to see you. Come in."

As she brushed past him, Alison was amazed to find the butterflies in her stomach had gone. Craig was as handsome as ever, but he seemed to have shrunk compared to the image of Chuck's broad shoulders and smiling face that had filled her mind for weeks.

"How are your arms?" Craig motioned to the cast on her right arm.

"Getting better." Alison shrugged. "What's new with you?" She perched on the edge of a flowered sofa.

"I have some exciting news." Craig's face lit up. "I decided to take your advice and study to become an actor. And I'm not going to wait for college—I'm going out to audition for a high school theater program in Vancouver. I'm sorry I didn't tell you earlier—I would have come to see you, but your mother said ..." Craig was stumbling over his words.

"Don't worry, I know what my mother said." Alison threw Craig a defiant look. "But she's in Japan, and anyway, I'm not going to let her decide who I can and can't see."

Craig relaxed. "Still the same old Alison."

"What does that mean?"

He looked embarrassed. "You know—used to getting your own way."

"I guess that's what Chuck thinks, too." Alison tipped up her chin. "That I'm still a spoiled, get-whatever-I-want kind of person."

"Chuck is pretty hard on you." Craig grinned. "Listen, do we have to talk about my big cousin?"

"No—"Alison paused, "actually, the reason I'm here is I was wondering if you could drive me out to the Bar Q to see Skipper. I don't want to ask Chuck."

"Sorry." Craig smiled sheepishly. "My mother took away my car privileges. I got ... a couple of speeding tickets ... wish I could help."

"That's okay," sighed Alison. "I'll figure out another way to see my horse." She looked curiously at Craig.

"What did your grandfather say when he heard you were going to be an actor?"

"That he always knew I was weird!" Craig laughed. "Secretly, I think he's pleased I had the nerve to do something on my own, not follow Chuck's lead all the time. I just hope I'm a success."

"Oh, you will be," Alison assured him. Craig was good-looking, charming, magnetic. It was just that the magnet's pull had been switched off where she was concerned.

As she left, Craig hugged her, cast and all, and kissed her gently on the lips. "Don't fall off any more horses," he said. "I want to see you in one piece when I come back."

"I won't," Alison murmured.

She walked out of the house and down Craig's front steps. A few weeks ago, a kiss from him would have set her heart racing. Now, it was just a nice good-bye.

"I feel suffocated, Grandmother," Alison complained not long after her visit to Craig. "Can we take another drive to the country?"

"You know I hate to drive." Grandmother Chant was loading the dishwasher.

"Here, let me do that." Alison nudged her tiny grandmother out of the way. "I'm getting good with my left hand."

"Just don't get your cast wet," her grandmother warned. She stood aside, letting Alison take over. Alison could only imagine how hard all the housework was for Grandmother Chant: cooking, cleaning, making beds. Back home, she had people who did those things for her. You have to admire her determination, Alison thought. If only she wasn't so bossy and sour about everything.

Alison tried again. "Look, it's a beautiful day. The poplars on the mountains will be golden, and we can stop in a little town and have tea …" She knew her grandmother's weakness for afternoon tea.

"Well …" Her grandmother almost managed a smile. "It would be nice to see something other than this miniature townhouse. I haven't been out for tea for ages." She dried her hands briskly. "I'll just slip into a dress …"

"You look fine!" Alison cried. They'd probably have tea in a diner on Main Street of a small town, and Grandmother would feel foolish all dressed up.

"Nonsense, it's always important to look your best." She glanced critically at Alison's T-shirt and jeans. "You could put on something nicer, dear."

Alison was about to bellow a protest when she remembered—patience. "I'll get a clean shirt," she compromised. After all, Grandmother might be more willing to drop in at the Bar Q after tea if she felt they were dressed for a millionaire's ranch.

Out at the Double J, Kristy rushed through the lunch dishes.

"I got to get out to Skipper," she muttered under her breath.

"You're spendin' too much time with that horse," Mike Jones said sternly from his seat at the kitchen table.

"Sorry, Pop." Kristy stared at the water in the sink. "But listen to him out there. He misses me."

Skipper Bug paced the paddock and whinnied loudly for Kristy. He was lonely and felt most secure and happy when he was with her. As long as she was close by, no mountain lions were going to pounce on him from above, and no steel gates would get in his way.

"Kris, it's no good," Mike said. "He's not your horse. You sold him for a lot of money, and it's a good thing we have it or I wouldn't be sittin' in this kitchen—I'd have lost the ranch." Mike was mad, not at Kristy, but at the whole situation.

"Alison can't look after him—she's hurt bad." Kristy turned her determined face to her dad. "I'm just trying to get him better so she can have him back as good as new."

"That's what you think you're doing!" Mike flung out his hands. "But how hard is it going to be givin' up Skipper all over again? Have you asked yourself that?"

"No ..." Kristy murmured. "I guess it will be hard, all right." She turned to the sound of Skipper's whinnying. "What else can I do, Pop? He needs me."

"You can call Chuck McClintock and tell him to come take that horse back to the Bar Q where it belongs. Go ahead now—do it!"

Kristy hung her head again and went to the phone. She could see her dad was mad, and that wasn't good for his heart, but sending Skipper back to the Bar Q would tear out her heart.

"I'd hardly call that a restaurant," Grandmother Chant sniffed as they drove away from the small diner on the main street of Milton later that afternoon. "But the tea was good."

Ten minutes later, they were coming up to Bighorn Road. "Turn here, please, Grandmother," Alison urged. "The scenery is so beautiful down this road."

"Why am I letting you talk me into this?" Her grandmother made a sharp left turn. "We'll probably get lost in the wilderness."

"I don't think so," Alison soothed. With every mile closer to the Bar Q they got, Alison was more determined to see Skipper.

The Joneses' place was just ahead.

"What a sorry-looking ranch." Her grandmother pointed to the tumbledown buildings. "How can people let their property get in such a state?"

"Sometimes they can't help it," Alison said, thinking of Mike Jones's heart trouble. She glanced past her grandmother at the Double J paddock and then looked again. "Grandmother, stop!"

Grandmother Chant hit the brakes so hard the car

slewed in the loose gravel. "What on earth is the matter with you, Alison?" she screeched. "Are you trying to put us in the ditch?"

"Turn down this lane," Alison begged. "There's something important—I have to see somebody." She had caught a glimpse of a big chestnut horse in the paddock and a blue truck parked nearby.

"Have you completely lost your mind?"

"No, Grandmother, please, there's a horse there I want to see. It will only take a minute."

"First it's a person you have to see, then it's a horse—oh! very well, but I hope you know what you're doing." The car bumped down the rough lane, with Grandmother Chant complaining all the way.

As they got closer, Alison was certain. It was Skipper Bug—her horse—in Kristy Jones's paddock. Chuck was there, too, with Kristy. Alison couldn't help it. She felt a surge of anger and jealousy that almost choked her.

CHAPTER 19

# CHANCE MEETINGS

"What are you doing here?" As she watched Alison stride toward the paddock, Kristy clung to Skipper's neck as if she wanted to fling herself on his back and ride away somewhere safe with him.

Never mind me! was on the tip of Alison's tongue to fire back. What's Skipper doing here? But the answer was right in front of her. Kristy and Skipper looked like a team, just the way they looked when she first saw them. Puny twelve-year-old Kristy could manage Skipper like no one else could. They belonged together.

Alison swallowed a lump in her throat. She wanted what Kristy had—that love between a horse and a girl—but it wasn't for sale. The trouble was, on paper at least,

Skipper was her horse. She'd paid twenty thousand for him and owed a chunk of that money to her mother.

Grandmother Chant had got out of the car and was fidgeting beside her. "I'm getting grass seeds in my panty hose. Is this the horse you came to see?"

"Yes, that's my horse. That's Skipper Bug," Alison said. "And this is Kristy Jones, who trained him." She gripped the fence rail. "How's Skipper doing?"

"F-fine," Kristy choked. "I'm walking him every day, and his leg seems to be healing."

Grandmother Chant shivered. "Do you mean to tell me this is the horse that charged into the gate—the horse that nearly killed you? I should think you'd never want to look at the creature again."

"It wasn't his fault," Alison said loudly, looking straight at Kristy. "It was mine. I should have known the gate would be shut. Anyway, Kristy is getting him back into condition."

Kristy stepped forward, leading the horse. "Pop says Chuck has to take Skipper back to the Bar Q. But Chuck says Skipper was off his food and sulky there. He says he's better off here, with me ..."

"We'll see," Alison muttered. She had just spotted Chuck, walking toward them, carrying a halter and lead rope. Her heart flopped over. He looked tall and strong and capable. How could she ever have thought he was ugly?

He stopped short, and his face turned red at the sight of Alison. "You look a lot better than the last time I saw you." He nodded in the direction of Skipper and Kristy. "I suppose you've come about your horse."

Pride choked off the words Alison had planned to say to Chuck. Not one word from him that he was glad to see her!

"It's fine that Skipper's here at the Double J, while I'm recuperating," she snapped at him. "Someone has to exercise him."

"Well, Mike wants me to take him back to the Bar Q." Chuck's voice was harsh.

"What does Kristy think?" Alison glared at him.

"I—I want Skipper to stay," Kristy managed to get out. She wrapped her arms around Skipper's neck again.

"Then go and tell your pop I want Skipper to stay too—I'll pay for his board and for you to exercise him, for me."

"Really?" Kristy brightened and dashed away to the house.

"You still think you can fix everything with money?" Chuck growled. "I guess you haven't changed, have you?"

"I'm only trying to help." Alison could feel her own face flushing. She wanted to scream at him.

"Ahem!" Her grandmother cleared her throat beside her.

"Sorry," Alison said through gritted teeth. "Grandmother, meet Chuck McClintock—he's the big hero who threw himself in front of Skipper when we crashed into the gate."

Her grandmother nodded. "Chuck McClintock? Well! I'm very pleased to meet you."

"Likewise, ma'am." Chuck reached out a thick hand to shake Mrs. Chant's. "I guess I won't load Skipper till I find out what Mike says." He exchanged a look with Alison. "As a matter of fact, I hope he says the horse can stay. Right now, she needs him as much as he needs her. Her mother took her little sister away to live with her in Edmonton."

"Skye's gone?" Alison gaped at him.

"Yeah, it's pretty lonesome for Kristy out here."

Alison gazed around the rundown ranch. She looked back at Skipper, gleaming like a shiny chestnut on the other side of the fence. He was hope and life for Kristy, she thought.

But at that moment, Kristy came stumbling back with tears rolling down her face. "Pop says no!" she cried. "I can't keep him—not even for a little while." She slipped through the fence to hug Skipper's neck once more.

"Why not?" Alison blazed. "I don't understand."

Chuck slipped the halter over Skipper's head and snapped on the rope. "Because Mike thinks it will be too hard for Kristy to lose Skipper again, if she gets used to him being here. He doesn't want her heart broken twice."

He turned to Kristy. "I'd better get him loaded," he said kindly. "It's best if you lead him to the trailer."

"What an unfortunate situation." Alison could see that her grandmother was touched. "Where are they taking the horse?"

"To Chuck's grandfather's ranch," Alison told her. "It's just down the road—a great big place." She was watching Kristy load Skipper into the trailer. She wanted to say she was sorry, but Kristy kept her eyes straight ahead and her shoulders high. Alison knew she was trying not to cry.

"Is his grandfather a McClintock, too?" her grandmother clutched her shoulder.

"Of course." Why was her grandmother so interested?

"Are we going to follow that young man to the ranch?"

"I'd like to spend more time with Skipper, find out about his condition," Alison said angrily, "but I don't think Chuck wants me there."

"Nonsense, it's your horse." Grandmother Chant opened the car door and got in. "I think we should go."

Alison stared at her grandmother. "You're right!" She got in the passenger side and they followed the trailer down the bumpy lane to the main road.

"Alison," her grandmother said severely, "what is that young man to you?"

"Nothing," Alison said bleakly. "I thought he was my friend, but he hates me. He thinks I'm a spoiled brat. In some ways," she confessed, "he's right, but I don't like him throwing it in my face all the time."

"You're too young for him, in any case," Grandmother Chant said.

"I'm going to be sixteen in a few weeks, Grandmother. Chuck's only eighteen," Alison pointed out, "but it doesn't matter, because we're not even friends anymore."

As they turned down the long driveway and approached Bar Q's beautiful house, Grandmother Chant straightened herself at the wheel. "It's a good thing I dressed," she told Alison. "One never knows whom one may meet."

Alison smiled to herself. Ever the snob, her grandmother knew enormous wealth when she saw it!

But she was totally unprepared for her grandmother's reaction when old Mr. McClintock came slowly down the front steps.

"Walter!" she whispered, grasping her throat. "Walter McClintock."

She opened the car door with a shaking hand and stepped out.

Chuck's grandfather rocked back on his heels, clutching the railing for support. "Elizabeth? Lizzie, is that you?"

Alison jumped out of the car and ran over to Chuck's pickup. "Something's happened," she gasped. "Look at our grandparents!"

CHAPTER 20

# OLD FRIENDS

"They know each other!" Alison exclaimed. "Look at them."

Grandfather McClintock was holding Grandmother Chant's hand. They stood gazing into each other's eyes without a word.

"It's like pouring water on two old prunes." Chuck was watching from his seat in the pickup. "I've never seen my grandfather straighten up so tall."

"Grandmother, too." Alison stared in disbelief. With her shoulders back and her chin tipped up, her grandmother looked like a young woman.

Chuck stepped out of the truck. "We better get those two old friends inside. They might stand there till the snow flies."

"Chuck, it's not funny. Let's not laugh at them …"

"But my grumpy old grandfather and your dragon of a grandmother?" Chuck shook his head. "What a crazy pair."

"Actually, it's not so crazy." Alison stitched together scraps of information. "My grandmother was awfully anxious to come to the ranch when she heard your name. And a little while ago, she told me she'd met a cowboy at Banff when she was a girl. He asked her to marry him, but something happened and they never got together. That cowboy must have been your granddad. I can believe she wouldn't marry him … she's so stubborn and proud …" Her voice trailed off at the look on Chuck's face.

"So is my granddad," he said. "I guess maybe we take after them."

Later, in the spacious log living room of the Bar Q, they heard the whole story.

"Walter's hair was just as red as Chuck's when I met him." Grandmother Chant looked up at Grandfather McClintock's bushy gray locks. "When I heard Chuck's last name and saw his red hair, I got quite a shock!"

She was sitting close beside Grandfather McClintock on the leather sofa, and Alison saw him pick up her hand and give it a pat. "That's right," laughed Walter. "I was a red-headed cowboy, working at the Banff Springs Hotel as a wrangler. I took the eastern dudes out for trail rides.

One of them was this little lady. The funny thing is, my hair's gone gray and my face is wrinkled as an old map, but Lizzie doesn't look one day older than she did then!"

Alison could not get used to Grandmother Chant being called Lizzie. She also couldn't get used to the constant smile on her grandmother's face after seeing it sour and disapproving for so long. Happiness had done more for her than all her face-lifts!

"She was the prettiest girl I'd ever seen," Walter went on.

Grandmother Chant beamed up at his powerful, craggy features. "But you were so scruffy-looking, and wild ..."

"And poor as a prairie chicken," he chuckled. "All I had was a dream of starting up the biggest cattle ranch east of the Rockies."

"And you've done it." Grandmother Chant waved around the lofty living room. "This beautiful house ... could you show me around?"

"It would be my pleasure." Walter stood up and offered Alison's grandmother his hand. They walked arm in arm out through the French doors to the terrace.

"I think they want to be alone." Alison flung herself down on a sofa. "Imagine, at their age! Grandmother's sixty-five."

"And Granddad's almost seventy." Chuck paced the pine floor.

"So, when they met, she was eighteen, and he was ..."

"Twenty-two or three," Chuck finished for her.

They stared at each other, trying to imagine their grandparents as young people, meeting for the first time—the rich society girl from New York and the poor Alberta cowboy.

"What would have happened if they'd got together?" Alison wondered. "I'd be a westerner!"

"That's not all. We'd be cousins!"

"Well, we're not. My father wasn't born until Grandmother Chant was in her twenties, I know that." Alison gazed out at the terrace. "I guess this explains why my grandmother's been so cranky all her life. She let the man she really loved get away."

"What about your grandfather?" Chuck asked. "Mr. Chant."

"He was a rich stockbroker, like my dad," Alison said. "He died pretty young, and Grandmother's lived alone for years, in the big stone house he built for her." She shuddered. "It's a cold, awful house—nothing like this one. I'll bet she was never happy."

"Same with Granddad." Chuck nodded. "His marriage to my grandmother didn't work out, and he's been on his own for years."

Alison looked down at her hands and took a deep breath. "If you don't mind, I'd like to talk about Skipper," she said. "How much would you say he's worth?"

Chuck stared at her with wide green eyes. "Don't tell me you're planning to sell Skipper?"

"Maybe. How much?"

"Well, not twenty thousand, that's for sure." Chuck started pacing again. "But then I don't think the horse was ever worth that."

"Never mind," Alison insisted. "How much is Skipper worth now?"

"Maybe four, five thousand, if he heals well." Chuck was glowering at her. "I can't believe you're talking like this."

"You don't understand ..." Alison tried to finish, but Chuck turned away.

"I think I do. You've ruined the horse and lost a lot of money. Now you're trying to make back as much as you can! You're your mother's daughter, that's for sure."

"And you are impossible!" Alison stood up, flushed with fury. She stalked out of the room, out of the house, to wait for her grandmother by the car. If he'd only listened, he would have known she was trying to find a way to get Skipper back where he belonged.

Alison's cast came off her right arm the following week. She shuddered at the sight of the shriveled skin, the slack muscles. It looked much worse than her left one.

"It's not coming along as fast as I'd like," Dr. Liu agreed when she saw the weakness in Alison's hand. "We need something to stimulate the nerves. You're a rider. How about getting back on a horse?"

"I'm not sure I could ride," Alison said glumly.

"Of course you could. They use horseback riding as therapy for kids whose bodies are weaker on one side than the other," Dr. Liu explained. "It seems to work because you have to be balanced to ride. Of course, you'd need a quiet, well-trained horse."

That rules out Skipper, Alison thought. Even if I planned to keep him, I couldn't ride him now. "Thanks, Dr. Liu," she said. "I'll think about it."

"Good luck." The doctor smiled as Alison left the office. "Don't despair. Remember—patience."

"Fine for her to say," Alison fumed out loud as she stalked down the hall to meet her grandmother. "She doesn't have a useless, shriveled arm!"

She'd have to think about riding. Her mother was due back from Japan in a few days, but Alison dreaded any discussion with her about horses.

"I can't believe you're even thinking about riding again!" Marion's dark eyes snapped. "I thought we were through with all that!"

"It was Dr. Liu's idea, not mine," Alison fired back. Her mom hadn't been inside the door two hours and they were already fighting.

"You're certainly not riding that dangerous animal, do you hear me?" Her mother's voice rose. They were nose to nose, mother and daughter looking so much alike, with their shiny dark hair and straight slender figures.

"No, Mom, I'm not going to ride Skipper. I'm going to sell him."

"Well, that's sensible, at least." Marion Chant paced the tiny living room. "We'll put the horse with a broker and get the best deal we can."

"It might be a horrible deal!" Alison shouted. "He's injured, and we have to find someone who'll look after him and get him back in shape. Skipper might go for dog meat if we send him to a broker."

"Then why, in the name of heaven, did we pay so much for that useless hunk of dog meat?" shrieked her mother.

"He wasn't useless until I ruined him. Anyway, he's improving. He's just not ready … oh! you don't understand." Alison could feel herself losing control.

At that moment, her grandmother walked briskly into the room. "Why don't we consult an experienced horseman on this matter of selling Skipper?" She faced her daughter-in-law. "Surely that would be better than all this screeching."

"That's what I said." Marion threw out her arms. "Get an experienced horse broker."

"I didn't say broker. We know someone much better than that." Grandmother Chant winked at Alison. "Walter McClintock."

Marion spun on her high heels. "That cowboy Alison was hanging around with? Never! I told him not to bother Alison anymore."

"No, Marion, not Chuck," Grandmother Chant said calmly. "His grandfather, Walter. We can ask him about selling Skipper at Alison's birthday party at the ranch."

"What birthday party?" Marion dropped into a chair. "What ranch?"

Alison knew her grandmother had been preparing a surprise for her sixteenth birthday the following week, but this was the first she'd heard about a party at the Bar Q. She slipped away to let her mother and grandmother battle it out.

As she climbed the stairs to her room, she caught a fragment of the crossfire.

"I can look after Alison now. You're free to go home, Mother Chant."

"Oh, I can't go home, dear. I've put the New York house up for sale. I'm buying a condo in Jackson Hole. Until the purchase is final, I plan to stay here with my granddaughter. She still needs someone to drive her to physiotherapy, and school, once she starts."

Alison didn't stay to hear her mother's astonished reply. She wondered what Chuck would think of her birthday party being at the Bar Q.

CHAPTER 21

# GOING ALONE

"Come to think of it," Grandmother Chant said to Alison in the kitchen later, "why don't you and I drive out to the ranch today and talk to Walter about your horse? There's no reason to wait until your birthday—I'll just get ready and call to tell him we're on our way." She hurried up the stairs like a girl.

Alison's mother gaped after her. "What on earth is going on with Mother Chant? She looks so ... different. And how does she know the McClintocks?"

Alison grinned. "You'll have to ask her" was all she said. Anybody could see the change in her grandmother. Even her wardrobe had changed. She'd visited a western boutique in downtown Calgary and bought herself fringed shirts and a pair of boots. When she came downstairs, she was actually wearing jeans.

"Let's go!" she cried, hustling Alison out the door.

"I'm right behind you, Lizzie," Alison said.

"Lizzie?" she could hear her mother's puzzled voice behind her. "You called her Lizzie?"

Once they were at the ranch, the real reason for the visit was clear. Chuck's grandfather had saddled a pair of horses for a trail ride. "It will be like old times," he told Alison's grandmother. "We'll take a nice quiet ride up in the pines."

"What about Alison's horse business?" Grandmother Chant asked. "We came to consult the expert."

Walter swelled up with the compliment. "Don't worry. Chuck knows as much about horses as I do—let him talk to Alison about Skipper Bug. You and I have a date."

As they rode off up a winding trail behind the ranch, Chuck shook his head. "I still can't get over it," he said. "My granddad is taking your grandmother riding."

"I never thought I'd see my grandmother on a horse—in a western saddle," Alison agreed. "Never in a billion years." She glanced sideways at Chuck. "Speaking of horses, can I see Skipper?"

"Sure."

Chuck's face was a mask, hiding his feelings. Was he still as angry at her as he had been the last time they met? Alison wondered.

Skipper was pacing around a small paddock, looking bored and restless. "I've been working with him every day," Chuck told Alison as they walked toward Skipper. "There's still a little tightness in his chest—he's not stretching out into his trot, and he's a bit lame in his left foreleg."

Alison hugged her own useless arm. "You make it sound hopeless."

"I don't think it is," Chuck reassured her. "He's making progress."

"Do you think he'll ever barrel race again?"

Chuck stopped. "Don't tell me you're thinking about racing him."

"Just tell me the truth—will he barrel race? It's important." Alison's dark eyes were fixed on his.

"I don't believe this!" Chuck stormed. "If you're thinking of racing this horse, I want no part of it." He wheeled away from her and stalked back to the gate.

Alison felt like a punctured balloon. She watched Chuck go, then turned to Skipper. Did the horse remember her? Did he remember that terrible moment when the gate loomed in front of him and there was no way to stop?

She took a cautious step forward. "Hello, Skipper," she said, to let him know she was there. He nodded, threw her one sideways glance, turned his glossy rump to her and went back to munching hay.

Alison sighed deeply. In horse language, that was like Skipper slamming a door in her face. There was no use forcing the issue—no use waiting to see if he'd come to her. She walked away and slipped back through the fence.

Chuck was mucking out a stall in the barn. "I'd like to

go visit Kristy." Alison raised her voice over the scrape of his shovel.

He dumped the shovel full of wet straw and horse manure in a bucket. His eyes scrunched up tight. "Whatever you say, your majesty."

Alison burned with the urge to say something nasty in return. Patience! she ordered herself. You have no other way to get to the Double J, except with Chuck.

Gravel spun as Chuck's dusty truck headed down the driveway for the Double J. He stayed silent and disapproving all the way to the Joneses'.

As they reached the leaning mailbox, Alison put her hand on his arm. "I'd like to walk from here and talk to Kristy and her dad alone."

Chuck jammed on the brakes. "Are you sure? The Jones family can be pretty hostile where you're concerned."

"Thanks for the warning." Alison felt the familiar swell of anger. As if she didn't know that! "Come back for me in half an hour." She jumped out of the truck and headed down the lane by herself.

With each step, she felt a little less sure this was a good idea. What if Chuck was right and they wouldn't listen? What if Mr. Jones came after her with a pitchfork?

Her footsteps flagged. What was she doing here? They hated her.

There was no one in the yard—maybe they weren't home. But the battered Double J truck was parked by the barn, so somebody was around. Alison forced herself to go up to the kitchen door and knock, even though by now she would have given anything to have Chuck's solid presence behind her.

Kristy opened the wood door and stared at her through the screen. "What do you want?"

Alison could see Kristy scan the yard for Chuck's truck or some other vehicle.

"I came by myself," Alison said. "I want to talk to you about Skipper."

Kristy started to slam the door in her face.

"No, wait, I have an idea!" Alison blurted. "I think I have a way you can get Skipper back."

The figure of Mike Jones loomed behind Kristy.

"What are you talkin' about?" he growled. "Do you think we'd accept charity from you? Even if you wanted to give my girl that horse, we wouldn't take it."

"Pop ..." Kristy howled.

"I don't want to give Skipper away!" Alison shouted. "If you'll just let me in, I'll explain."

"Pop, please," Kristy begged.

Mike stood back from the door. "I don't know why I'm doin' this," he grumbled. "You've brought nothing but misery to my family ... but come in."

Half an hour later, Alison was waiting by the mailbox when Chuck drove up.

"How did it go?" he asked as she hopped in.

"Okay," Alison said, not looking at him.

Chuck glanced at her. Alison's proud face had a look he'd never seen before. "Aren't you going to tell me?"

"Not till I know for sure. Can we go back to your place to meet my grandmother now?"

"Sure." Chuck turned the truck around. "The two old lovebirds should be back from their trail ride." He peered at Alison. "Do you know about this birthday party they're cooking up for you?"

Alison took a deep breath. "I heard something ..." Chuck sounded so unenthusiastic—as if a birthday party for her was the last thing he cared about.

"Sounds like a big fuss," he grumbled. "Granddad wants me to wear a tux."

Alison suddenly had a picture of Chuck with slicked-down hair and a red face, stuffed into a tight black suit. He'd hate that.

"Tell your grandfather not to bother," she said. "I'd hate to see you have to go to any trouble over my birthday."

CHAPTER 22

# SWEET SIXTEEN

"Of course you have to have a birthday party." Liz Chant looked shocked. "It's a day that comes only once in your life. You're sixteen, no longer a child. As of today, you can get a driver's licence, be your own person, go out on dates."

"I know all that," Alison sighed. She'd been dating since she was fourteen, but this wasn't the time to bring that up. "But does my party have to be this huge extravaganza at the Bar Q?"

"Walter and I have done so much work arranging everything!" Liz looked crushed.

"All right." Alison threw up her arms. She knew this party was just another excuse for her grandmother and Chuck's grandfather to get together—it was really all about them, not her.

"But I can't wear this dress." Alison held up the gossamer pink and white party dress her grandmother had picked out for her. It had a frilly hem, fringes and beads, and flowing sleeves.

"It will look fabulous on you," her grandmother insisted. "Take it from me, dear, it doesn't hurt to dress up once in a while."

"But this dress!"

"Just try it on ... for me?"

Alison gave in and slipped the dress over her head. It floated around her.

"Now, these white cowboy boots ..." Her grandmother handed her a pair of boots in the softest white leather.

"Grandmother!"

"Try them." Her grandmother cocked her head to one side like an eager little bird as Alison pulled on the boots. "There! My beautiful granddaughter." Alison could see tears in her grandmother's eyes.

Alison turned and looked in the mirror. Her image stared back at her, surprised. This was a different person. Her short dark hair and slender neck were set off by the ruffles, her waist accented, her long legs looked longer with the boots and the full skirt. "It's ... nice," she stammered. "But it's not me."

"It's you, at sixteen, dear," her grandmother said softly. "Go ahead and take it off if you like—I know an old woman's taste isn't the same as a young girl's. I've seen you in it, that's enough."

Alison sighed. There was no way out of this "sweet

sixteen" party, she realized. Her grandmother had too much invested in it. Alison had a sudden flash of Chuck in a tuxedo. They might as well look ridiculous together. She'd wear the dress.

When Alison walked into the living room at the Bar Q, she saw that the furniture had been removed, except for a few chairs near one wall, and a long white table near the other. At the end of the room a stage had been set up. A drum set and music stands stood waiting for the musicians. "Live music?" Alison breathed.

An enormous "Happy Birthday, Alison" sign, surrounded by dozens of balloons, floated from the ceiling. Large vases of flowers glowed on the pine staircase. Alison felt embarrassed. This was way too much. The room was so empty, and silent.

But as she and her grandmother and mother entered, "SURPRISE!" rang out, and people emerged from every doorway. Musicians took the stand and swung into "Happy Birthday." Uniformed wait staff appeared with trays of food and drinks for the table.

Alison gaped. Coming down the open staircase was her cousin Becky, her Aunt Laurie and Uncle Dan—her whole Mustang Mountain family.

"Becky!" Alison raced across the floor in her high-heeled boots and flung herself into her cousin's arms. "How did you get here?"

"Your grandmother arranged everything." Becky laughed. "We came down yesterday, but we weren't allowed to call you. Are you really surprised?"

"Blown away!" Alison laughed. "Wow! Look at you!" She held Becky out at arm's length. She was wearing a blue dress that brought out the color in her cheeks and the blonde highlights in her hair.

"Your grandmother, again." Becky grinned. "She wouldn't let me say no."

"I know," Alison laughed. "But she's really changed. I have so much to tell you ..."

Alison was swept up at that moment in a hug from her Uncle Dan and Aunt Laurie. "Our turn," her aunt said.

Then it was her mother hugging her sister Laurie, and everyone hugging each other. Suddenly, Alison felt a tap on her shoulder.

It was Chuck.

He looked so stiff and embarrassed in his white shirt and black tux that she felt sorry for him. "I invited some other people to your party," he murmured. "I hope you don't mind." He broke off as Alison turned to see Kristy Jones, her little sister Skye and their father in the doorway. "Skye's mother let her come home," Chuck whispered in Alison's ear as they approached. "And Kristy told me you're selling Skipper to her on an instalment plan for a fair price."

"You know?" Alison gasped.

"Yeah, and I'm sorry I didn't catch on to what you were trying to do. I think it's a great idea." He paused. "I guess I haven't been listening to you lately. Or looking, either. Wow! That dress."

Alison knew that this was really Chuck's way of saying he was sorry for all the misunderstanding between them. She turned to greet Kristy and her dad. "I'm glad you came," she said. "Did Chuck tell you he thinks Skipper will be able to race again—as long as I'm not riding him, that is." She glanced over her shoulder at Chuck.

"He'll race." Kristy's eyes were shining. "And we'll win races again, and I'll pay you back with the prize money we win, even if it takes forever!"

"It won't," Alison said. "Skipper's a great horse. And you're a great rider, Kristy. You're going to be one of the best barrel racers in the world someday, I just know it—"

"My pop's all better now," Skye interrupted. "So Mom said I could come home." She spun around on the shiny floor. "Like my dress?"

"It's beautiful." Alison laughed.

"I still feel funny about takin' Skipper back." Mike looked embarrassed.

Alison shook her head. "It's all right. I should never have bought him in the first place. I have a friend who says some things can't be bought."

She grinned at Chuck. He smiled back. "There's one other guest at this party you haven't met," he told her.

"He's a bit shy, so he's waiting out on the terrace. Come meet him."

"Craig?" Alison asked, then laughed. "No, can't be. Craig's not shy."

Chuck led her by the hand to the large french doors. Outside, the cool autumn night was starry, and glimmering lanterns lit the wide stone terrace.

Alison heard the clop of hooves and saw the shape of a horse coming into the light. A beautiful horse, with a fine, noble head, warm brown eyes and a dark glossy coat. He was one of the most powerfully built quarter horses Alison had ever seen, a bay with a black mane and tail and ... a white cloverleaf on his forehead.

"Lucky?" Alison gasped. "This can't be Lucky Ralph. He's so ... filled out!"

"You haven't seen him for a while," Chuck laughed. "Once he started eating seriously, he grew into that big head of his."

"He's gorgeous." Alison stepped forward to stroke Lucky's smooth, muscled shoulder. "But what's he doing out here in the garden, loose?"

"Like I said, he came to your party," Chuck laughed again. "He's turned into a big pet. And Granddad's turned into a real softie—he lets him have the run of the place."

He stroked Lucky's face. "I heard from Lizzie that you need a quiet horse for therapy on your arm ... therapeutic riding, they call it? Well, I hope you'll accept Lucky as a sixteenth birthday present from me to you, and I hope he'll be lucky for you. He's the gentlest, quietest-going horse I've ever known."

Alison threw herself at Chuck. He wrapped his sturdy arms around her. "Thank you, Chuck," she cried. "It's the best birthday present ever." That's not true, she thought. The best birthday present is this hug. She felt giddy with happiness.

They left Lucky grazing on the lawn and went back inside.

The music was playing and the lights were dimmed. Everyone was dancing. Chuck undid his bow tie. "Want to dance? I'll try not to step on your feet."

"Sure." Alison was surprised to discover that Chuck was light on his feet. But I shouldn't be surprised, she thought. He dances like he rides.

Around Chuck's shoulder she saw Mr. McClintock dancing with Becky, Mr. Jones dancing with her mother, and her grandmother dancing with Kristy. Then the musicians broke into a waltz and Mr. McClintock and Grandmother Chant took over the floor, swirling around and around in perfect time to the music.

"Look at them go." Chuck shook his head in wonder. "I never knew the old man could waltz."

"They look like they've always been together," Alison murmured, "like they belong." Like Kristy and Skipper, she thought. Like me, and Chuck—maybe!

Later, there was more food and more presents, and toasts to Alison's being sixteen. "We have another announcement to make," Walter boomed out, as though he was addressing a large crowd, instead of a dozen people. "Elizabeth and I have had a lot of fun planning this party. I suppose it's a dress rehearsal for another party we hope to be hosting in the very near future, when this lovely lady becomes my wife." He put his arm around Alison's grandmother and beamed down at her.

"Like I thought." Alison grinned to herself. "This party's really for them." But somehow, she didn't care. It was great Lizzie had found her cowboy after all these years. Maybe they could be friends now—she and her grandmother.

"Let's go outside," she whispered to Chuck. "I want to see Lucky." The truth was, she realized, she suddenly wanted to be alone with Chuck.

In the darkness at the far side of the terrace, Lucky Ralph was now munching the fall flowers. His white cloverleaf stood out against his dark face and they could see it bobbing up and down.

Alison moved closer to Chuck, standing quietly beside her on the terrace in his white dress shirt and dark tuxedo jacket. "You rescued Lucky," she said. "Are you sure you want to give him up?"

Chuck nodded. "Lucky was never my horse. I rescued him because he needed help. Someday, I'll find another horse I like as much as Copper, but not yet."

He laughed at the sight of Lucky peacefully munching pansies. "That horse is definitely yours. He's got a mind of his own, just like you. And don't forget," he added, "Lucky has some speed. Once your arm is better, you can get him barrel racing, if you like."

"Racing." Alison sucked in her breath. "You're right—he might make a terrific barrel racing horse. We'll have a great time, once my arm gets strong again. I hope you'll take us to lots of races."

She turned to look at Chuck. The lanterns on the terrace threw off a soft glow, highlighting parts of his face, throwing others into shadow. I'm sixteen and my real life is beginning, she thought with surprise. I have a new horse, named Lucky, and a friend, named Chuck.

Excitement and the October night made her shiver in her thin dress.

"Actually, there are other places I'd like to go with you, besides barrel races," she told him.

Chuck took off his jacket and wrapped it around her shoulders. "What other places?"

"Movies, concerts … I'm sixteen now." Alison's dark eyes flashed. "My grandmother says I'm officially old enough to date."

Chuck stepped closer. "Me?"

"Who else?" Alison laughed.

**1** *Sky Horse*
ISBN 1-55285-456-6
Meg would do almost anything to get to Mustang Mountain Ranch, high in the Rocky Mountains. She wants a horse so badly. A sudden storm delays the trip and begins an adventure that takes Meg, her friend Alison and Alison's cousin Becky far off the beaten track. To reach Mustang Mountain, they'll need every scrap of courage they possess.

**2** *Fire Horse*
ISBN 1-55285-457-4
Meg, Alison and Becky are alone at the Mustang Mountain Ranch. When two horses go missing, the girls and their friend Henry set out on a rescue mission. Caught in a forest fire, they save themselves and the missing horses with the help of a wild mustang stallion.

**3** *Night Horse*
ISBN 1-55285-363-2
Returning to Mustang Mountain Ranch for the summer, Meg, Alison and Becky meet Windy, a beautiful mare about to give birth to her first foal. Meg learns a secret too: a bounty hunter has been hired to kill the wild horses in the area. When Windy escapes the ranch, the girls move to protect the mare and the wild horses they love.

**4** *Wild Horse*
ISBN 1-55285-413-2
On vacation at a ranch in Wyoming, Meg, Alison and Becky have a chance to ride wild horses. Alison doesn't care to participate. Her mood threatens the vacation. She changes, however, when she discovers a sick wild horse. As hope for the sick horse fades, Alison must conquer her anger and come up with a plan to save it.

**Rodeo Horse**  **Brave Horse**  **Free Horse**

### 5 *Rodeo Horse*
ISBN 1-55285-467-1

Alison and Becky prepare to join the competitions at the Calgary Stampede. Becky wants to find out more about Sam, the mysterious brother of a champion barrel racer. Meg meanwhile is stuck in New York, longing to join the Stampede. An accident threatens the girls' plans. Or was it an accident?

### 6 *Brave Horse*
ISBN 1-55285-528-7

A phantom horse, a missing friend, a dangerous valley filled with abandoned mine shafts ... Not exactly what Meg, Alison and Becky were expecting on vacation at the Mustang Mountain Ranch. Becky had expected a peaceful time without her annoying cousin Alison. Alison had expected to be traveling in Paris. And Meg had planned to meet with Thomas. Instead, the girls must organize a rescue. Will they be in time?

### 7 *Free Horse*
ISBN 1-55285-608-9

New adventure begins while Meg and Thomas care for a neighbouring lodge and its owner's rambunctious 10-year-old stepson, Tyler. The trouble starts when Tyler opens a gate and lets the ranch horses out. In his search, Thomas discovers that someone is catching and selling wild horses. Could it be Tyler's brother Brett and his friends? A hailstorm hits and Thomas fails to return to the lodge. Can Meg and Tyler find Thomas and save the wild horses?

available Fall 2005
9 *Dark Horse* ISBN 1-55285-720-4

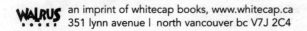

**WALRUS** an imprint of whitecap books, www.whitecap.ca
351 lynn avenue | north vancouver bc V7J 2C4

# ABOUT THE AUTHOR

As a child, Sharon Siamon was crazy about two things—books and horses.

Born in Saskatoon, Saskatchewan, Sharon grew up in a farming area of Ontario. She learned to ride by coaxing a farmer's big workhorses over to rail fences with apples, then climbing on their backs and riding bareback till they scraped her off under the hawthorn trees that grew along the fence. She wished for a horse of her own and read every horse book she could find.

Sharon has been writing books ever since for kids who dream of having adventures on horseback, among them *Gallop for Gold* and *A Horse for Josie Moon*. The Mustang Mountain adventures began with a wilderness horseback trip through the Rocky Mountains. Sharon's friends in the exciting fields of barrel racing and endurance riding have kept the adventure going. So far, the Mustang Mountain books have been translated into Norwegian, German, Finnish and Swedish.

Sharon writes back to all the fans who write to her at her email address: sharon@sharonsiamon.com.